Lorilyn Roberts

A YOUNG ADULT FANTASY

SEVENTH DIMENSION

BOOK 2

THE KING

LORILYN ROBERTS

Visit Lorilyn Roberts' website at http://LorilynRoberts.com

Copyright ©2014 Lorilyn Roberts
Published by Roberts Court Reporters

Cover design by Lisa Hainline
Edited by Katherine Harms and Lisa Lickel

Taken from the Complete Jewish Bible by David H. Stern. Copyright © 1998. All rights reserved. Used by permission of Messianic Jewish Publishers, 6120 Day Long Lane, Clarksville, MD 21029. www.messianicjewish.net.

Library of Congress Control Number 2014914518

ISBN: 978-0989142694 (e-book)
ISBN: 978-1500785888 (print book)

For names of persons depicted in this novel, similarity to any actual persons, whether living or deceased, is purely coincidental.

LORILYN ROBERTS

TO MY JEWISH ANCESTORS

AND

JEWS WHO ARE STILL SEARCHING FOR THE MESSIAH

LORILYN ROBERTS

ACKNOWLEDGEMENTS

Special thanks to the following beta readers for making THE KING BOOK 2 better than it would have been without their insightful suggestions:

Deborah Dunson, Sally Ann Bruce, Kendra Stamy, Gregg Edwards, Hannah Bombardier, Lilly Maytree, Rachel Liankatawa, and Felicia Mires.

AUTHOR'S NOTE

Readers will have no trouble enjoying and understanding THE KING BOOK 2 even if they have not read THE DOOR BOOK I. I hope, though, readers will want to know Shale's story, too.

"A spiritual kingdom lies all about us, enclosing us, embracing us, altogether within reach of our inner selves, waiting for us to recognize it. God Himself is here waiting our response to His Presence. This eternal world will come alive to us the moment we begin to reckon upon its reality." – A. W. Tozer, THE PURSUIT OF GOD.

Contents

CHAPTER I DEATH

"P lease, God, don't let him die!" I cried.

General Goren's face turned blue as the medic and nurse rushed into the room.

The nurse barked orders. "Start chest compressions. One, two, three, four—" seconds passed.

"No pulse," the medic said.

After applying gel, the nurse placed the defibrillator pads on his bare chest.

"All clear," she yelled.

We stepped back and waited.

The heart monitor remained flat.

"Again," the medic said.

On the second attempt, General Goren's eyes fluttered open.

A faint hope stirred in the room.

The death cat stood in the doorway. The nursing home mascot had never been wrong—maybe just this once. I wanted to yell at the cat to go away.

"Daniel," a voice said faintly.

I leaned over and squeezed the General's hand. "Yes, I am here."

His eyes met mine. I drew nearer, avoiding the wires leading to the equipment. His breathing was labored. I was thankful the nurse and medic didn't insist I leave.

"There is something I need to tell you," he said faintly.

I shook my head. "No, save your energy. You don't need to tell me now."

"I must," he pleaded. "You must know."

I glanced at the medic and nurse. He was in no condition to talk. "Know—what?"

He squeezed my hand reassuringly. "You saved my life at Synagogue Hall."

"What?" The man must be hallucinating.

The General continued. "May, 1948—hospital in Jewish Quarter."

"No. It was someone else. I'm Daniel Sperling, son of Aviv, a volunteer at the Beth Hillel Nursing Home. I'm seventeen years old."

"Let him talk," said the medic. He lowered his voice, "In case he dies."

"Don't say that," I whispered.

The cat stood in the doorway—watching.

General Goren pulled me closer. "No, Son. It was you. They carried me in on a stretcher. I had a collapsed lung. The Arabs had burned everything but the hospital. The flames—cries of children—horrible. Mothers and fathers—all gone. The children—" he stopped, unable to continue.

I reassured him. "You did the best you could. Everyone did."

General Goren flinched. "Dr. Laufer and Dr. Riss had a flashlight. Nurse Tzviah tried—" his voiced cracked again. "I told them not to waste any more time on me, to help the others."

I'd never heard this story. The war hero rarely talked about those weeks in Jerusalem. Despite his successes many years later, he apparently never forgot that night.

"The reinforcements didn't arrive in time. We held out as long as we could."

"Forgive yourself."

Tears welled up and he coughed. His eyes stared and the medic shocked him again.

"We have a heartbeat, a faint one," the nurse said.

Should I leave so he could save his strength or stay and let him finish?

General Goren said, "I must tell you this before I'm gone."

"I'm listening."

The room became quiet. The only sound was his weak, raspy voice.

"You had a scar on your forehead. You walked over and touched me. The pain left. I cried out to the nurse—I wanted to know who you were—but you were gone."

My hero had mistaken me for someone else.

"Thank you for saving my life," the General said. "I didn't tell you before because I didn't think you would believe me."

I squeezed his hand.

"God has great plans for you. You're an angel." The old man stopped breathing.

"He's gone," said the medic.

We checked the monitor. The war hero who had survived so many battles was no longer with us.

I ran out the door, tripping over the cat. I stopped and turned to face the poor creature. "Sorry," I muttered.

His gray eyes stared into space, but the cat's purrs reached my ears. I reached down and picked him up. Stroking his head gently, I leaned over and kissed him. Couldn't the blind animal have been wrong just this once?

CHAPTER 2 THE GIFT

T hree Weeks Later

I trudged up Mount Zion to the Old City reciting my prepared speech. "Dear Mother, I'm not going back to the Family and Youth Treatment Center. Crazy people don't know they are crazy. Patients who punch walls and claim to see monsters in the dark will make me crazy if I stay, if that's what you want—" no, that sounded disrespectful.

I approached the Prayer Plaza. An Orthodox Jew wearing a fur hat sat in front of the Western Wall. He, along with others deep in prayer, faced the most sacred wall in the world—the only remnant from the temple still standing.

I passed a bookstore selling Jewish T-shirts, jewelry, and photos of Mount Zion. The closer I came to home, the more I hurried. Familiarity put me at ease, though tensions ran high in the streets.

The Family and Youth Treatment Center forbade TVs. Too much bad news, they said. When was there not bad news? I would not go back—my day pass would be permanent, even if I had to run away.

The sign at the gate, Jewish Quarter Street, greeted me. I walked faster, anticipating the surprise on the faces of my mother and sister. Of course, I would have to explain. I'd worry about that later.

I heard the approach of running feet behind me on the stone walkway. Someone called my name, "Daniel, wait."

I stopped and turned. A young girl about my age ran up to me. I didn't recognize her, but she seemed to know who I was.

"Hi," the young girl said, catching her breath.

I searched my memory. "Do I know you?"

"I don't think so. I'm Lilly Ruston, a friend of Maurice."

How did she know Maurice? A brilliant mathematician, he always helped me with calculus.

She dropped her eyes, as if now embarrassed by our impromptu meeting.

"Were you looking for me?"

She groped for words. "Yes. Daniel, we've been praying for you, about the loss of your father and now General Goren."

"Thank you."

An awkward silence followed. I didn't know what to say to the stranger.

She edged towards me. "I have something to give you. I hope you will take it. I mean, if you don't want to, I'll understand, but God told me to give this to you."

I looked down at the book in her hand and read the title. *Jewish New Testament*, translation by David H. Stern. Should I refuse it? I'd never read a book like that.

"Thank you," I offered. "I might look at it." I lied.

"It's written for Jews," she said.

"We aren't practicing Jews, except for the holidays, like Hanukkah and Yom Kippur."

"I wanted you to know we're praying for you. God told me to give you this book," she said again. Her voice trailed off, as if she had lost the courage to say more.

I checked my watch.

"Are you returning home? I mean, have you been discharged?" she asked.

So she knew I had been at the Treatment Center. "Yes, I'm going home." I looked around. "Where do you live?"

"In the Armenian Quarter. My father is a professor at the Institute of Holy Land Studies."

"Oh." I remembered seeing students outside the building on several occasions, but I didn't know much about the college.

"He teaches Arabic."

6

"Can you speak it?" I asked.

She laughed. "No. I speak English and a little Hebrew."

"You speak Hebrew well," I corrected her.

A brisk wind blew her long brown hair over her shoulders.

Under different circumstances, I'd have been interested in her, but I wanted to get home. "Well, thanks for the..." I searched for the correct name of the book.

"New Testament."

I held it awkwardly. "What was your name again?"

"Lilly Ruston. Don't tell anyone I gave it to you."

"I won't. Thanks for your prayers."

"Maurice said you were a good friend."

I nodded and started towards the Jewish Quarter.

"Stay safe," she hollered as I walked away.

CHAPTER 3 DINNER

As I approached our apartment, I remembered my father. If only things had been different. He was a passionate businessman and treated the Arabs with respect. In fact, they were his best customers. His family had done business with them in Syria for years.

He knew the risks. He trusted them too much, we used to tell him, especially when Syria disintegrated into splinter factions.

Why would someone want to kidnap him—the conclusion the authorities came to when all the leads came up empty. Even though the police never found his body, we assumed he was dead. Two years later, the wound festered, unable to heal.

Our history was full of such sad stories—everyone had their own version. Jews had more versions than everyone else—the historians were right. We were different.

I opened the gate to the side alley.

I had never known a time when war was not a possibility. Soldiers carrying guns on the streets were commonplace. Even women had to serve—our survival as a nation depended on everyone being a Zionist. Despite the past, though, I didn't want to live anywhere else.

Recently military planes had increased practice runs in the wilderness of Judea. There they could perform military maneuvers without disturbing the civilian population.

When I was younger and camped with friends in the remote area, I would look up and see the birds fly over and wait for the sonic boom. That's how I learned sound traveled more slowly than light.

As I climbed the stone steps to our apartment, lingering doubts returned. Perhaps I should have stayed at the halfway house. I'd brought some sanity to the poor souls, if not even a little humor. Just as birds perceive the arrival of winter before the first frost, the collapse of peace talks and military maneuvers pointed to war.

I glanced at the *Jewish New Testament*. Too bad a dumpster wasn't nearby so I could throw it away. I set the book by the front door.

When I poked my head inside, my mother was cooking over the stove. I slipped by her to say "hi" to Martha. My sister was reading a book curled up on the sofa. When she saw me, she jumped to her feet. "Daniel!"

I wrapped my arms around her. "So, Mother's turn to cook, huh?"

Martha laughed. "I get to do the dishes."

Mother ran into the living room. "Daniel, when did you get here?"

"Just now."

A confused look spread across her face. "Did they discharge you?"

"Sort of."

Tears weld up in her eyes. "Oh, Daniel, I missed you." She rushed over and hugged me.

I forced myself not to get emotional. We often didn't see things the same way, but I loved her as any good Jewish son would.

The aroma from the kitchen awakened my hearty appetite. "Am I in time for supper?"

Mother smiled. She had pulled up her hair in a bun and wore a long, cotton, flared skirt and modest green blouse. "Sit and chat with your sister. Only a few more minutes."

Martha motioned for me to join her on the sofa, but I chose the chair instead. I sat and leaned back, rubbing my hands along the leather arms. I closed my eyes briefly, thankful to be home. When I opened them, Martha was smiling.

My sister wore tight blue jeans and a white cotton blouse—no doubt an expensive name brand, though I wouldn't know the difference if it were a cheap counterfeit. I tried to see what she was

10

reading, but couldn't—probably a hot romantic book by an American author.

The view of Mount Zion through our dining room glass doors looked the same as always. Everything was as I'd left it a few weeks earlier. The old photograph still hung on the wall behind the leather sofa, taken at Yad Vashem when Martha and I were young. Mother's grandparents had been victims of the Holocaust and she had insisted we visit the museum.

My guitar sat in the corner. I was the only one who was musical in the family.

We chatted about school and business, avoiding the political situation. Martha whispered, "I bet you left on your own, didn't you?"

I put my finger to my lips. I couldn't fool her, but I'd rather not confess to my mother until I had to.

"How is the business?" I hoped to change the subject to something less edgy.

Martha caught on. "It's okay. Well—sort of, except for Moshe doesn't—"

"What's the problem?"

Martha shook her head.

Ever since our father's disappearance, we had depended on Moshe to restock our fabrics and textiles from Syria. Few were willing to make the perilous journey, but we paid him well.

"Food is ready," Mother said. "Let's eat."

The dining room table brimmed with hot food—my favorites, turkey and gravy, steamed white rice, avocado salad, and my favorite pastry, Boureka. Martha said the blessing, one of the few religious traditions we kept.

Mother watched me intently. "I'm glad you're back, though no one told me you were being discharged."

I knew the topic would come up. I was still a minor.

I set down my fork and wiped my mouth with a napkin. "I need to tell you," I began.

Mother's eyes got wide. "What's the matter?"

"I got a day pass, but I'm not going back."

"How did you get a day pass without a chaperon?"

11

"I stole it."

"What do you mean, you stole it?"

"I was depressed, but that place is for lunatics. Perhaps a visit to the rabbi would have been sufficient, just someone to talk to."

"Daniel, I don't know a rabbi well enough to send you to one. That part of my life is over."

Mother could forsake her religion but she couldn't take the Jewishness out of her blood. Bitterness now filled that hole.

Not embracing our heritage had cost us. If we weren't God's people, who were we?

"You know they will be looking for you."

"If you want me to go insane, send me back."

My caring nature was a doubled-edge sword. Everyone knew I wanted to be a doctor, but after being so depressed following General Goren's death, she questioned my ability to become one.

I turned to Martha, as if asking her for support. She listened attentively.

"Mother, just let them know Daniel came home," Martha suggested.

I moved the salad around on my plate. "I feel something is about to happen. And I want to be here when it does."

Mother shook her head. "Don't say things like that, Daniel. Why do you scare me? One minute I want to believe you are okay, the next minute you worry me with your preoccupation with the future, about what might happen."

I lashed back. "Just because I feel things more than others doesn't mean I'm crazy." My words were ignored. I'd always had a better relationship with my father. My mother, Kitty—as much as I loved her—frustrated me with her inability to see other people's viewpoints.

She was silent as she dug into her food. Taking a few bites without speaking dissipated the tension. Finally she said, "Maybe it's best. We have some business news we need to discuss."

"Like what?"

"I'm sure you realize now how difficult it would be to get into medical school."

Was that a question or a statement? I glanced at Martha. "What do you mean?" Was this what she started to tell me?

"Moshe can no longer make the trip to Syria. He believes it's too dangerous and isn't willing. He fears the aggression will spill over into Israel any moment—that the recent events are far more serious and likely to lead to war. We need someone to take his place and take over the family business."

Take over the family business? "I can't do that—I'm not old enough, and I still have three years to serve in the IDF."

"I know," she said reluctantly. "I'm thinking down the road. We can find someone on a short-term basis, if we pay him enough."

She wanted me to sacrifice my dreams for her security.

"You want me to take over the family business instead of becoming a doctor?"

Mother looked away to avoid eye contact. "How could you ever be a doctor? I mean, your reputation—"

"What reputation?"

"You're too unstable, Daniel. And anyone who has a mental breakdown is not going to be admitted into any medical schools in Israel."

Anger rose within me. "That's a pretty judgmental thing to say."

Mother stabbed her knife into the turkey. "You don't know what suffering is. Not until you've—"

I glared back. "Not until what?"

Mother didn't need to tell me. The flames of Auschwitz were in her eyes. Her grandparents were murdered and her mother was left an orphan.

Her only picture of them she kept by her bedside. Probably her most cherished possession, though Martha and I were a close second. Not that she loved us less—but we were her children. She had never known her grandparents.

Martha interrupted. "We don't have to discuss this tonight. Daniel just got back. Let's wait until tomorrow and talk about it. You can call the Treatment Center and let them know he's home."

Mother nodded. She wiped her face as if to wipe away the heated conversation.

What sorrow did she carry? Perhaps I was more like her than I admitted.

"Would anyone like some tea?" Martha offered.

"I would love some," I said.

CHAPTER 4 CONFLAGRATION

T he French doors were open and a gentle breeze lifted the aroma from my mint tea. A deep red painted the sky as the sun arced below Mount Zion. Memories stirred from happier times.

Mother collected the dishes from the table and carried them to the sink. "Since you're back, you should check the mail."

"Anything important?"

"You got your letter from the IDF."

My rite of passage.

S leep eluded me. After an hour of tossing and turning, I remembered the book Lilly gave me. Why had I agreed to keep it? I slipped out of bed and tiptoed to the front door. When I opened it, cold air gushed into the hallway. I grabbed the book and returned to my room. Flipping through the pages, I stopped to read a couple of lines.

"It was during those days that Yochanan the Immerser arrived in the desert of Y'hudah and began proclaiming the message, 'Turn from your sins to God, for the Kingdom of God is near.'" If Lilly asked me if I'd read any of it, I could say yes and wouldn't be lying.

I slipped the book under my pillow. Mother and Martha would never find it unless they changed my bed sheets. They hadn't done that in years. A tree branch rubbed against the apartment window as the wind kicked up. I stared at the ceiling. A sense of uneasiness haunted me. The clock said 2:00 A.M. Sleep finally came but not for long.

I woke with a start when the bed moved and I heard several explosions. A flash of light pierced through the partially opened blinds. I pulled up the shades. The streets were dark except for emergency lighting, but beyond the city walls, the sky was bright. The sound of barking dogs bounced off the stone walls amid wailing sirens.

I ran down the hallway. The floor moved again. Mother and Martha met me and we rushed into the dining room. When we pulled up the blinds, glowing streaks of fire covered Mount Zion. Fire balls shot up into the sky. Smoke made it hard to see and flames engulfed the mountain.

Scorched trails up and down in shades of red and orange glowed. I stared in disbelief. The Temple Mount and the Dome of the Rock were not visible, but neither was anything else—hidden by the flames.

"The ground moved," Martha said.

I shook my head. "We've never had earthquakes around here. Maybe terrorists attacked."

Below the mountain, emergency vehicles blocked traffic, making cars turn back. The traffic heading away had snarled to a crawl.

Neither of us wanted to mention the unthinkable. I finally asked, "If the Dome of the Rock is gone, do you know what that means?"

"The Israelis would never do anything to the Temple Mount," Mother said. "That would be an act of war."

"I didn't say we did anything, but something happened."

"The Arabs will blame us," Martha said.

I clicked the remote to the T.V. "No power."

"I already tried to turn on a light," Mother said.

I ran back to my room to get the computer. The battery would last for a couple of hours. I waited for the desktop to appear on the screen and clicked on Google. Nothing happened.

"We have no Internet," I said.

Martha turned on her iPhone. "My God!"

I learned over her shoulder. "What is it?"

"An earthquake. It says the Dome of the Rock is burning."

Martha flitted through several tweets on her twitter feed. "Rockets have been seen—over Northern Israel. They are headed towards Tel Aviv and Jerusalem."

"Can they get through the iron dome?" I asked.

Martha shook her head. "I don't know."

Mother stood. "We'd better go to the safe room."

Before we could move, another explosion rattled the apartment. This one felt closer, within a few hundred meters.

Mother's face turned white even in the darkness.

Martha reached for her. "What is it?"

"I feel weak, like I'm going to faint."

"Sit down," Martha said. "Here, let me help you."

I stared at the fiery mountain. "This is more than just an earthquake. How long would it take for a missile to reach us?"

"From Syria?" Martha asked.

"Don't talk like that," Mother said.

Another explosion shook the floor. Screams from outside the building cut like a knife. At least one explosion was close enough to be inside the walls of the Old City.

"No," Mother screamed, "Not again."

"Hamas?" Martha asked.

Mother's eyes bulged. "We're going to die."

The last blast was close. It was too late to leave our apartment for a safer place. Where would we go anyway?

The sirens continued like a stuck needle on a record player.

Martha's voice trembled. "We need to go to the safe room."

"I see fire," Mother sobbed. "The fires of Auschwitz." She carried the scars like a badge of courage.

"This is not Auschwitz. This is Jerusalem." I leaned over and rubbed her tense shoulders. I wanted to pray for the first time since

17

our father went missing, but I couldn't. I wasn't sure I believed in God anymore. The wounds were too deep.

Martha's phoned beeped. "We need to go to the safe room," she said again.

We had prepared the room a few months earlier when the political situation deteriorated. The essentials were in a plastic carton—three bottles of water for each of us, several energy bars, as well as the recommended emergency supplies: A small flashlight, matches, whistle, pencil, paper, pocket knife, rope, compass, sleeping bag, battery-operated radio, garbage bags, wet naps, and toiletries.

I snatched the laptop computer as well as my Kindle, though I'd forgotten to charge it the night before.

The only window in father's office faced Mount Zion. We had argued about whether we should seal it. We didn't. I could still picture him at his desk working late into the night. He lived in his own world of chaos—selling to the Arabs when other Jews wouldn't.

The last shipment he had sent ahead of his return, but the package didn't arrive until days after his disappearance. The box sat in the corner, unopened—two years later. That we never found his body left me embittered.

Stashed in the other corner were three gas masks and additional food and water.

"Don't forget the phone charger," I told Martha.

Mother sat on the cot and Martha and I shared the floor mat. We spread out our sleeping bags. The sirens continued. Intermittent barking dogs sent my mind wandering where it shouldn't.

"How long should we stay in here?" Martha asked.

I shrugged.

Martha propped herself up with a pillow. I could barely see her face in the moonlight through the window.

"At least we don't have to use the gas masks," I said.

Martha shifted on the floor. "Not yet. I'd hate to suffocate using one."

"You won't suffocate if you put it on correctly."

"Some people did during the Gulf War," Martha argued.

18

"Have you ever used one?" I asked.

"No," she said glibly. "You know I wasn't born until a year after that."

Mother changed the conversation. "What time is it?"

Martha reached over and checked the iPhone but didn't say anything.

"What is it?" I asked.

"It's worse than I thought."

"What is? What are you looking at?"

Martha clicked a few more times on the keypad. "I have a text message from a number I don't recognize. It's using the Hebrew code word Homat Barzel."

She switched back to her twitter feed. This is from the Haaretz Newswire. 4:15 A.M. Tel Aviv hit with drones. Damage to the Diona nuclear reactor feared. The Azrieli Towers have collapsed and are on fire. Dozens presumed dead."

Mother lamented. "We should have moved to the countryside after your father disappeared."

Martha continued. "The Kikar Hamedina Square was struck and the IDF's control command complex—hit also. Not sure how severe."

"What about here?" I asked. "What is all the fire that we saw, the smoke—I can smell it."

"I don't know," Martha said. "Here's another report. The *USS Abraham Lincoln* was attacked on its way through the Strait of Hormuz."

Mother looked at me. "Daniel, try the radio again."

I did, but heard nothing but static.

"Here, let me try the Israeli News," Martha said.

Rubbing my tired eyes, I scooted closer. I wished my iPhone hadn't been stolen. I could find things quicker than my sister could.

"Apparently the earthquake hit a gas line and blew out a section of the Armenian quarter—many casualties."

"We have lots of friends in that area," Mother said.

Lilly Ruston came to mind. Why didn't I get her address?

"We need to pray," Martha said. She glanced around the room.

I opened a breakfast bar and swallowed some water. An uncomfortable silence followed when no one offered.

"We should take turns sleeping," Mother said.

Martha nodded.

I dozed, vaguely aware of the faint whisperings of my mother and sister. I awoke around eight. The cold room gave me goose bumps. I pulled a sweater out of the box and slipped it on.

"Have you heard anything?" I asked.

Martha shook her head.

Mother's eyes looked swollen.

"Both of you need to sleep," I said. "I can stay awake now."

Mother reluctantly agreed. She pulled the covers up around her. Martha's eyes were already closed.

I heard grating sounds, like people moving things. Maybe emergency workers were attempting to dig people out of the rubble.

Why did I lose my iPhone? I would have to pay for my next one. I flipped through Martha's phone looking for emergency updates. News was either being withheld or the stations had no power to broadcast. I texted several friends whose phone numbers I could remember. I figured they were waiting it out also.

I dug through our box of stored food. Since I never thought we'd eat the stuff, I made little effort to get things I liked. The pistachios and peanut butter would provide protein. I swallowed some water to get rid of the aftertaste.

With all the sirens, an emergency update was due. I flipped on the computer, but still had no Internet. The best information came from tweets scattered around Jerusalem and Israel.

I glanced at Martha and my mother. Could this be the start of World War III? I grabbed a gas mask. The other two masks shifted in the pile making too much noise. I froze and waited. Thankfully, neither of them was disturbed. I picked up my mother's iPhone and texted Martha a message, "Be back shortly."

After closing the door quietly, I walked into the dining room. Mount Zion continued to burn. Several roads were unpassable and part of the mountain had collapsed.

It must have been an earthquake. The tremor underneath the mountain probably caused a shift in the plates. Emergency vehicles and street traffic clogged the road below the mountain.

I lifted the gas mask over my head and latched it. The unit was bulky and uncomfortable. I strode towards the front of the apartment and cracked the door. Smoke filled the narrow alleyway making it difficult to see. Footsteps approached and something brushed against my leg. I looked down to see a trembling brown and white dog. Her fearful eyes tugged at my heart. I patted her on the head and she wagged her tail expectantly. I checked for a collar but she didn't have one. How would I ever find her owner?

If chemicals were used, would she be alive? I didn't think so, and I took solace that fewer lives would be lost. I headed to the epicenter of the Old City with the dog nipping at my heels. She was probably afraid of losing me. At Zion's Gate, more chaos confronted me.

Israeli soldiers blocked the entrance. "You can't go in there," one of them said.

He had on a gas mask. I was glad I wore mine.

"You need to go home. We fear more explosions, or go to a safe room."

St. James Monastery in the Armenian quarter lay in ruins. What about all the priceless books? Martha loved to hang out there and read.

Prior attacks filled my mind. We always questioned if this was the big one. The Old City hadn't been attacked since 1967. We would never surrender Jerusalem to the Arabs again.

A sheet covered a darkened corner of the alleyway. I imagined dead bodies hidden underneath it. A soldier stood guard.

"I'm looking for a friend," I said.

The guard didn't move. "Some of the injured have been sent to Hurva Square. The synagogue has been converted into an emergency room. Many casualties have been reported. Right now, you need to go home, Son, and stay out of harm's way. Take your dog with you."

"Yes, sir." I didn't realize the dog was still following me.

The soldier wasn't going to allow me to enter. Men with bewildered looks wandered by. Not everyone wore a mask. Women sobbed. I started to head back to our apartment and then stopped. I had to know if Lilly was okay.

I turned towards Hurva Square. The new synagogue stood where the old one had been before its destruction in 1948. The Arabs burned it to the ground. The medics had treated General Goren in the makeshift hospital in the synagogue after he suffered a near mortal wound. Too many had died to keep Jerusalem from the Arabs. In the end, the Jews failed. That we would use it again as a hospital felt surreal.

The dog stayed with me as I walked through the hazy streets. The cafes were closed and the usually crowded souvenir shops were deserted. The thick smoke showed no sign of dissipating.

I arrived at the synagogue and told the dog to wait outside the door for me. I paused before entering—suppose she was hungry. I reached into my pocket and pulled out an energy bar. "Here's something to eat."

She greedily gobbled it down.

I grabbed a discarded plastic cup from a table and poured her some water from my water bottle. She lapped it up. The smoke had made her thirsty.

Patting her on the head, I said reassuringly, "I'll be back in a few minutes." She whimpered and crouched on the steps.

She was too obedient not to belong to somebody.

When I entered the synagogue, the worship center buzzed with activity. Cots lined the walls with injured and hurting people. Cries drifted from several beds. Medics and nurses were everywhere. A quiet calm existed but the intensity of the suffering was enormous. I took off my gas mask and set it in a corner.

A man came up to me and handed me blankets. "Give these out to those who need them."

"Yes, sir." I handed out the blankets to anyone who asked. I looked into the eyes of the hurting—I wished I could offer hope. Did God even care? If he did, why did he allow this to happen?

I felt a tug on my pants and looked down at a young boy. He held a small teddy bear in his arms. "Do you know where my mommy is?"

I crouched down to his eye level. "No, I don't. When did you last see her?"

The young boy looked away. "I don't know. It was a long time ago."

"What about your dad, do you know where he is?" I asked.

"He died," he said unemotionally.

Did he understand what that meant? "How do you know that?"

"The man put a sheet over him."

I embraced the boy in my arms. How could I find his mother?

Then a young woman approached. "David!"

The little boy let go of me and ran into her arms. I rejoiced over their reunion before I looked into the eyes of another victim.

"Thank you," his mother said. She appeared too overwhelmed to say more, covering her face with her hair. I watched as she carried the boy out of the synagogue.

CHAPTER 5 SUFFERING

T he wounded kept arriving.

"Help me," a voice cried.

I rushed over to an elderly man on a cot. His face was cut and pieces of shard glass clung to his matted hair. His bandaged hands crisscrossed his stomach, which appeared distended from internal injuries. I crouched in front of him as his arms and legs shook.

"My wife and daughter, do you know where they are?" he rasped.

I shook my head. I laid a blanket over his body to keep him warm. "Can I get you anything?"

He closed his eyes. Was it from pain or did he die? If only I were a doctor.

He reopened his eyes and said weakly. "My wallet—pocket. Picture. Please find my wife and daughter."

I dug into the man's pocket but came up with nothing.

"Other one," the man said.

I went around to the other side of the makeshift bed and stuck my fingers inside his front pocket. I pulled out what appeared to be a wallet. When I opened it, several credit cards fell out, along with a photograph. I stared at it. "Is this your daughter, Lilly?"

"You know her?" He asked.

I nodded. "Where should I look first, like—where do you live?" The man didn't respond. I felt for a pulse. I didn't want to leave him. I looked around for help. I didn't see any medics except for a young woman dressed in a white coat.

I ran to her. "Can you help? A man is severely injured."

I pointed to the back row where he lay.

The nurse shook her head. "All the patients are triaged. Those at the back are not deemed salvageable."

My heart sank at her unsympathetic words.

"We are concentrating on the ones we can save. We're just trying to make those souls comfortable."

"No, you must come," I pleaded. "He's—he's a friend of mine. This is his family." I showed her the photograph from the man's pocket. "They will be looking for him."

The nurse sighed. "I'll be with you in a minute—after I start this IV."

She pointed across the room. "Someone started a wall up towards the front where people are posting photographs of the missing."

Then she returned to the patient in front of her, a young girl not much older than me.

I bolted to the front. Dozens of photographs had been hastily hung—of children, mothers, fathers, grandparents, brothers, and sisters—of someone. Many had scribbled notes with names, emails, and phone numbers to contact. There were even a couple of pictures of dogs and one cat—a black and white one that reminded me of the nursing home mascot.

I stole some scotch tape and tacked the picture of Lilly and her mother among the others. I wrote on the top—father is on a cot in the back.

I hurried back to find the nurse leaning over Lilly's father. She was checking his blood pressure and temperature.

"This man needs a doctor if we are going to save him."

"So there is a chance?" I asked.

"If you're the praying type, I would pray. I'll find a doctor." She brushed past me.

I knelt beside the man and spoke gently. "I posted the picture of your wife and daughter on the front wall. Hopefully they will see it and be here shortly."

The man nodded. "I'm an Arab," he said.

An Arab? Lilly had given me a Christian Bible. How could she be a Christian if he were an Arab?

The man closed his eyes. Guilt over my sudden lack of empathy for the man convicted me. An Arab kidnapped my father. I couldn't leave him, though—not now. I'd stay with him for Lilly's sake.

A few minutes later, the nurse reappeared with a doctor. I moved out of their way.

The doctor did a quick assessment. "I examined this man when the medical team brought him in," the doctor said. "I felt his injuries were too severe. Is he your father?"

I shook my head. "He's the father of a friend."

The doctor felt the man's abdomen. "Keep him warm, and we'll schedule him for surgery. We have a van with supplies on the way. If he can live a few more hours, he might make it."

"Thank you, sir."

The doctor turned to the nurse and gave her some orders I didn't understand.

Then he spoke to me, "Through that door are some stacked cots that were brought in earlier. Set them up wherever you can find room. Another bomb exploded and more casualties are on the way."

"Yes, sir." I hurried towards the back. The door opened into a dark hallway lit only by emergency lights. A few cots remained, stacked along the walls. I gripped one but something caught my attention.

An old door appeared in the hallway. Rough-hewn wood framed it and the door seemed out of place in the recently rebuilt synagogue. The studs beside the door were loose and unattached. A cool breeze blew through the square opening at the top.

I leaned on the cot suddenly feeling weak. Resting to catch my breath, I peered through the window of the door. Beyond it, a bright light shone through the darkness. Could this be an illusion, the work of the enemy, attempting to break into the synagogue?

I edged closer. I expected a barrage of bullets, but the light drew me. I pushed open the door and the harsh light temporarily blinded me. I blinked a couple of times. When my sight returned, I saw a wooden chair floating about a foot off the marble floor. I had never seen a chair quite like it—cubical and plain with severe edges, a straight back, no arms, and a solid wooden base.

In slow motion, I edged towards it—drawn to it because it was all I could see. Where was I? I felt that I was stepping out of my familiar world and entering another. I touched the floating chair and it remained stationary, as if glued to an invisible floor. I climbed into the chair and once seated, vibrations filled the room. The green light faded into darkness.

CHAPTER 6 TIME WARP

The vibrations stopped almost as swiftly as they began. The thickness of nothingness wrapped invisible tentacles around me. I couldn't see my hands and I dare not make a sound. Had I been captured? Who had this kind of technology? My eyes adjusted as the blackness lifted. I felt as if I were leaving a movie theater and walking outside—except this was an otherworldly light tinged with bluish-green effervescence, the kind of hue seen in icy artic waters.

A voice said, "Daniel G. Sperling."

I jumped at the sound of my name. Goosebumps crept up my arms. A very large man wearing a black robe appeared. He approached me carrying an open book that looked ancient. "I don't see your name."

"What book is that?" I asked. "And who are you?"

The man glared, "Prisoners are forbidden to ask questions of their captors."

Another very tall man appeared. His robe was a different color. The shimmering reflection varied between white and gray-blue—a strange color I had never seen.

"The book is incomplete. Not everyone's name has been written in it yet."

The first man shook his head. "He's a Jew."

"Their time has not yet come. You are too soon," the second man replied.

The two argued back and forth. I couldn't perceive if they were good or evil or if they were even human. I decided the men were Israel's enemies that had just attacked us. Didn't they have better things to do than play mind games with me?

The man in the lighter-colored cloak said, "Each man is entitled to a fair trial, and he hasn't had his yet."

Those were the last words I heard before something happened that I could not explain.

The outline of familiar objects—like trees and bushes panned into view. Further away people that looked like trees were walking on a dusty road. Then my eyes adjusted. A crow perched on one of the stone columns of the overhanging portico screeched loudly.

Had I been exposed to a hallucinogen? I couldn't remember what had happened, nor did I recognize my surroundings.

I saw no synagogue or anything resembling the Old City. Instead, I appeared to be sitting in a small portico on a stone walkway that led to a stone building. The Hebrew sign at the front entrance said "Jacob's Inn."

Sitting beside me were two men. One man appeared to be slightly older. Their clothing was similar to what the Bedouin wore—a tunic with an outer cloak. They were speaking in Aramaic.

I glanced at my clothes. I was wearing a tunic and cloak like theirs—of earthen colors. My sandals were also strange.

One of the two men sitting near me said, "You don't look so well, fellow. Are you all right?"

I blinked. "I don't know. Where am I?"

The two exchanged glances. The older man knelt in front of me, examining my face. "I think you need a doctor," he said. "You have a cut on your forehead."

"I do?" I put up my hand and felt blood. "I don't remember cutting myself."

"Let me get the doctor." The man grabbed his walking stick and hobbled inside Jacob's Inn.

The younger man who had been sitting with him made idle conversation. "My name is Ami." He reached out his hand.

"I'm Daniel." I shook his hand back.

"The doctor will be here in a minute," Ami said.

"Thank you."

"So who do you think the man is?"

"What man?"

"You didn't hear our conversation?"

I shook my head.

"Oh, I thought you were listening. He calls himself Yochanan the Immerser. He is down by the Jordan River telling the people the kingdom of God is near." Ami waved his hand. "'Repent, repent,' he says. He immerses followers in the Jordan River."

Where had I heard something similar? I shook my head. "Sorry," I said, "I don't know him."

Ami squinted. "How could you not have heard of him? Everyone has been talking about the strange prophet who lives in the wilderness and eats locusts and wild honey."

I heard footsteps and turned to see a middle-aged man approaching. His white outer cloak and intelligent eyes reminded me of a twenty-first century doctor. He clutched a small leather bag in his hand. When he placed it on the bench, I noticed the instruments looked like antiques. I winced at the thought they might possibly be used on me.

The man smiled warmly and reached out to shake my hand. "Hello, I'm Doctor Luke."

"Hi," I said. With those garden tools, what kind of doctor was he?

"Looks like you cut yourself on your forehead. Can I take a look?"

I nodded.

Dr. Luke leaned over and wiped the blood away. He then examined the wound. "Does it hurt?"

"Just stings a little."

"It's not bad. I will clean it and put a bandage on it. You'll be as good as new."

"Thank you."

"What's' your name?"

"Daniel, son of Aviv."

"How old are you, Daniel?"

"Seventeen."

"Have any family around here?"

"No. They all live in Jerusalem."

"Oh. So you're visiting?"

I nodded.

"Jacob, son of Aviv, owns the inn. Not related to him?"

I shook my head. "I don't think so."

He applied a salve. "All done. Let me know if you need anything else."

"Do I owe you anything?"

Dr. Luke shook his head. "I help those I can. If people want to do Tzedakah, I appreciate the almsgiving."

"That's kind of you," I said. I was still trying to remember what I did to cause the cut.

He put his instruments back in his bag. "You should probably change the bandage tonight to keep it clean."

I nodded. "Thanks again."

He walked back inside Jacob's Inn. The others gave a respectful wave as the doctor passed. He exuded the air of a physician. His garb was far from anything kosher for an Israeli hospital in 2015, but his demeanor was a cross between a scientist and a priest.

I glanced around the rundown building. He must not have cared for worldly pursuits to hang up a shingle in this two-star inn—a place apparently frequented by the lowly and the poor. The other men near me were either infirm or old.

Farther away, a cripple sat alone, save for a cat draped over his clubbed feet. What a remarkable resemblance to the cat at the nursing home, all black except for white paws and a black circle on his front shoulder. Briefly, my heart ached as I remembered General Goren, my mentor and hero.

32

My eyes returned to the man who originally spoke to me. He and his younger friend, Ami, had rough beards, long scruffy hair, and smelled. I suppose I'd start smelling too when my deodorant wore off.

"What's your name?" I asked the older man.

"Levi. From the tribe of Levi."

"That makes sense," I replied.

The old man laughed and tugged on his beard. "Not used to seeing such clean-shaven young men around here."

I wasn't sure I could grow a beard.

"So where are you staying?" Levi asked.

"I don't know. I haven't thought that far ahead."

Ami nodded. "It's a long trip from Jerusalem. You should check the inn and see if they have any openings."

I stood and stretched, realizing I hadn't eaten much since the night before. Hunger pangs made me feel weak. I walked across the portico and entered the front door.

Inside Jacob's Inn, I found a large lobby with an adjoining room with wooden tables and chairs. Apparently, it also served as a dining hall. Men and women were eating from old ceramic plates with their hands. Why weren't they using utensils—ugh, so unsanitary to eat with one's hands.

An attendant at the long counter greeted me. "Can I help you?"

I started to dig into my pocket for my wallet and then realized I wasn't wearing my jeans. I hated to appear stupid. "I need a room tonight, but I seem to have lost my money." I pretended to check my cloak.

"I'm sorry," the man said with genuine concern. "Where did you last have it?"

I shook my head.

The man took pity on me. "What's your name?"

"Daniel, son of Aviv."

The clerk retrieved a document from the shelf and glanced through it. He raised his eyebrow. "We have you booked for tonight, Daniel, son of Aviv. Your room has been prepaid."

"Prepaid? By who?"

"It says benefactor."

I stared at the clerk. Maybe he was making up a story so as not to embarrass me.

"Here," the clerk said. "Can you sign in and I will give you your key."

I examined the writing. The document showed what the clerk said, "Paid in full by benefactor." Why did the paper feel like parchment made from animal skins? I signed the paper mystified.

The clerk handed me a large wooden key—another antique.

"Your room is through the door, the third on the right."

"Thank you," I said. "And this is just for tonight?"

"Yes, sir. One night."

I'd worry about tomorrow night later.

I searched for my room. Maybe I'd even lie down.

I rattled the key in the door and found the room to be clean but earthen, containing just the bare necessities. A bed was in one corner layered with heavy coarse blankets. A small wooden table with an oil lamp and chair occupied the other corner. The lamp reminded me of those I'd seen in museums or shops where tourists frequented.

I glanced around. Where was the bathroom? Did I have to share one with other people? Well, it was free, so I couldn't complain.

I sat on the bed questioning my sanity. Had I become like the patients in the treatment center? They lived in their own worlds of reality. I shook my head. No. I wasn't dreaming—somebody brought me here. If this were my creation from insanity, I wouldn't have invented this kind of world. I'd have gone to Nepal and hiked the Himalayan Mountains.

Maybe I was a prisoner and my captors wanted information from me. The Aramaic was a different dialect, at least not anything I'd heard spoken in Syria.

I tried to remember what happened before I arrived. I remembered going into the hallway to retrieve the cots and seeing a strange light.

A weird thought hit me. I stood and checked the door to make sure no one had locked me in from the outside. Then I got down on my hands and knees and examined the floor—even underneath my

34

bed, looking for a camera or eavesdropping equipment. I studied the walls—nothing but illegible graffiti.

I noticed an opening underneath the table. I checked inside the hole and saw a scroll. I pulled it out and unrolled it. The document was a map of Israel, though many names were different. I recognized some of the towns, like Jerusalem. I sat on the floor and studied it. The date on the map was 3790. I assumed this was using the Hebrew calendar.

If it was the year 5775 using the Hebrew calendar, that meant I was back in time two thousand years. That couldn't be—or could it? I did a quick math computation. Converted into the Gregorian calendar from the Hebrew calendar, that meant it was about 30 C.E.

I threw the map on the floor disgusted—or perhaps more petrified than disgusted. How did I get here? No! This was insane. Besides, I'd rather be a prisoner of war than be here. Then the military would search for me. I knew what happened in Israel at that time—with the Roman occupation and an itinerant rabbi who claimed to be the Messiah. I didn't want to be here.

I sat on the floor shaking. "Why God, why here, why now? What happened to me that I can't remember?" The walls did not answer me.

A moment of revelation—I wouldn't find any hidden cameras or microphones. Even if I went back to Jerusalem, my family wasn't there and wouldn't be for two thousand years. How could I figure out how to get back to 2015 when I didn't know how I got here?

I picked up the map and stuffed it back in the cubbyhole. What was I to do? I could sit around and mope—no, I was too frustrated to do that. I sighed. Perhaps there were clues. Maybe someone could help me. I'd go back out to the lobby and listen, eavesdrop on conversations. Until I could figure out how to return to my world, I would have to learn how to live in this one.

Reluctantly, I joined the others out in the lobby where most of the inn's guests seemed to congregate. Dr. Luke sat at a table by the window with another man. I walked over hoping not to appear intrusive. When I sat nearby, the two stood. The other man shook

35

Dr. Luke's hand. When he left, Dr. Luke turned to me and joined me at my table.

"How long are you going to be here, Daniel?"

I scratched my ear. "I don't know." I picked at the food crumbs on the dirty table. Hunger pangs filled my stomach.

Dr. Luke studied my face. "How is your forehead?"

I reached up and touched it. "It's much better. Thank you for bandaging it."

"Make sure you keep it clean until it heals."

"Yes, sir. I will." I took a deep breath before continuing. "Doctor Luke, you seem to be a very busy doctor. I am hoping someday to become a doctor."

"It's a fine profession for a young Jewish boy. Make sure you study hard in school."

I searched for the right words. "If you need help, Doctor, I could use a place to stay for a few days, until I head back to Jerusalem."

Dr. Luke's face brightened at my suggestion. "In fact, I do need help with one small task that no one wants to do, and it's difficult for me to find the time."

"What's that?" I asked.

"It's sorely needed."

"Tell me what you need done."

Dr. Luke studied the tabletop and looked sad. "They appreciate anything anyone does for them. Their life is very difficult."

"Whose life is very difficult?"

"The leper colony outside the city gates. If someone doesn't bring them food, they die."

"Oh, the lepers." What could be so terrible about visiting them? Unless I caught the disease, but couldn't it be cured?

"I would be happy to help you with the lepers," I found myself saying a little too eagerly.

"Are you sure?" Dr. Luke bit his lip. "I mean, you don't go inside the colony. You leave the food outside the gate."

"Sure. I can do that."

"Great. I'll let the inn know to bill me for your room and board." Dr. Luke seemed delighted that this burdensome task was taken care of.

I nodded and smiled, grateful that I wouldn't starve.

CHAPTER 7 WHIP OF ROME

A pproaching hoof beats interrupted our conversation. Alarm appeared on the faces of the inn's guests. The clerk cleared his reservation desk and locked up the hotel documents in the cabinet. I glanced at Dr. Luke. He was peering out the window.

"The Romans," Dr. Luke said. "What do they want here?"

I knew the Romans and the Jews did not like each other.

A flock of birds dispersed outside the inn, leaving an ominous foreboding in the air. Soon horses filled the street and five Roman soldiers dismounted, tied up their animals, and hastily scattered in different directions.

The street was empty. The locals had sought shelter when they heard them coming. The soldiers entered the store across the street and exited when they didn't find what they wanted. One recklessly overturned a fruit stand. The fruit scattered in the street, a week's worth of wages for one farmer.

Two stampeded into Jacob's Inn. Though all the other patrons had fled the porch, the crippled man sat on his mat, unable to escape. No one thought to help him.

One of the guards approached the paraplegic and kicked him. The man fell over, moaning in breathless gasps. Suddenly the cat I had seen before vaulted through the air and landed on the soldier's back. The surprised guard's attention turned from the paraplegic as he reached up to seize the maniacal creature off his shoulder. Then

39

the cat leaped through the air and disappeared. I winced. Dr. Luke closed his eyes, as if he were praying. No one in the lobby moved, hoping the men would go away.

What if the Roman soldiers entered the inn?

Soon the guards swaggered inside, their armor clanging. The Centurion glared around the room. When he saw me, he pointed, "Grab him."

The other guard stormed towards me. I swallowed hard as my head swirled. Why was he coming after me? I started to throw up.

Dr. Luke held up his hand. "Wait a minute. What's the problem? Why do you want to seize this young boy?"

The Centurion stated impatiently, "A young man fitting his description looted the treasury yesterday in Ramallah. He was observed heading towards Dothan—on foot."

"This young man works for me," Dr. Luke said. "I'm sure you're mistaken. He feeds the lepers."

When the guards heard the word "lepers," they backed away, wanting nothing more to do with me. "Mistaken identity," the Centurion said. He glanced around at the frightened guests. "Have a good day." The two Romans left as quickly as they came, issuing no apologies for their actions.

When the intruders were gone, Dr. Luke ran outside to check on the crippled man. I noticed the others in the room edged away from our table. They wanted nothing to do with me either.

The life of the lepers before antibiotics—the living dead, the abandoned, victimless faces of souls who died a little each day as limbs withered and deformity took over.

I stood and followed Dr. Luke outside. He was hunched over the poor man. Tears filled the doctor's eyes. The cripple lay motionless on the ground.

"He's dead," said Dr. Luke.

Now I hated the Romans as much as I hated the Arabs. Why had God abandoned us?

"Does he have a family?" I asked.

Dr. Luke shook his head.

A few minutes later, the dead's man body was carted off, though I didn't know to where and I was afraid to ask. The portico

40

seemed empty without the cripple's presence. Burdened that I had made no effort to talk to him earlier, I vowed to be more caring.

Once things returned to normal, I asked Dr. Luke, "Why did you do that?"

We were sitting in the portico alone. Evening approached and the cooks were busy preparing the food.

"Do what?" Dr. Luke asked.

"Why did you speak up for me to the Roman soldiers? I mean, how did you know that I didn't steal the money?"

Dr. Luke looked away for a moment pondering my question. "Someone who is willing to feed the lepers wouldn't steal money from the Romans."

I nodded. "I understand now."

Dr. Luke reached over and patted me on the shoulder. "Let's get something to eat."

CHAPTER 8 THE LIVING DEAD

The next morning I made my first trip to the leper colony. The outcasts lived in a cave beyond the city gates on the outskirts of civilization. I fed the donkey and suited him up with as much as he could carry. Dr. Luke warned me to look out for robbers. They were known to hang out near the entrance to the colony and raid what kindhearted folks left.

The colony was at the mercy of others, hidden behind the walls of secrecy. Forbidden to be seen even by family members, they were worse off than zombies.

I packed boiled fish, bread, honey, nuts, pomegranates, olives, grapes, and figs. No one knew how many lepers were in the colony, but Dr. Luke sent food every couple of days.

I left at sun-up to avoid detection. The streets were empty and the air was cool. I had never been to Dothan because the town was a military zone and inaccessible. I never imagined I would see the small town in the first century.

The place had a curious history. The Tanakh said the Armenians trapped Elisha in Dothan. As enemies of Israel, they tried to capture Elisha but the chariots of fire defeated them.

The Merkabah, fables about the heavenly throne chariot, were forbidden to be read during regular synagogue services—not that we ever attended, but I was fascinated with the chariots and the mystical stories surrounding the village. I wished I could see one of the chariots of fire.

I arrived at the outer gates within an hour. The cave was nearby and marked with the sign "leper colony, stay away." A narrow trail hidden from the street led to the lepers. Overgrown vegetation and spindly vines wet with morning dew made travel difficult on the donkey. The trailed ended at a small natural clearing.

After unpacking the supplies, I rang the bell on the donkey to alert the lepers. A small pair of eyes peered at me from behind some vines at the cave entrance. He moved out of view when he realized I saw him. I knew they wouldn't approach as long as I was present, but I wanted to make sure the food wasn't stolen.

I reluctantly led the donkey back up the trail. I lingered at the top, hoping to catch a glimpse of one of them. I hadn't seen any robbers, but I was ready to shoo them away if one appeared.

A few minutes later, a young child came out of the cave. He grabbed some figs and ran back inside. I chuckled. He didn't look sick, but Dr. Luke said healthy kids were expected to live with their leprous parents if they had no other family. A man appeared with a cloth draped over his head and face.

What would happen if I came out of hiding? Would he run away? I'd have given away my favorite guitar to have five minutes on Google to look up leprosy. Soon a few more lepers appeared to carry the supplies into the cave.

Without warning, robbers appeared. The lepers fled. They had no standing in the community to defend themselves. Filled with anger, I came out of hiding.

"Get out of here," I yelled at the villains.

One of the thieves absconded with the pomegranates. He was too far away to catch and tackle.

I got in the second bandit's face. "Go away, you thief."

He didn't move.

I yelled again, "I'm a leper," and I shoved him backwards.

When he heard my words, he took off.

Out of breath and gulping in air, I calmed myself. I heard movement in some nearby branches. Two eyes were peering at me.

"I won't hurt you," I said.

The person came out into the opening and removed his head scarf. Lesions covered his deformed face. His nose and lips curled up to the left, now permanently displaced with scarring. The man's heart-wrenching plight touched my soul.

"I don't see any leprosy on you," the man said.

44

I tried to make eye contact again, but the man refused to look at me.

"I don't have leprosy," I confessed. "I didn't want those marauders to steal the food I brought."

"Go away," the leper said, "before this death comes to you and I am burdened with making you sick."

"What's your name?" I asked.

The gulf between us grew.

I asked again. "What is your name?"

"Simon. Now go away."

"My name is Daniel."

A silence followed.

A few minutes later, another man walked out holding the hand of a young boy. I recognized the lad as the one who took the figs. His eyes were bright.

Leprosy covered the cheeks and forehead of his apparent father, though not as seriously as in Simon. My eyes returned to the disfigured man. I studied him, aware I was probably the only non-leprous person who had seen him in years. Would I shame him, run away in disgust, or fear?

Suddenly something hit Simon in the head and knocked him over. He grasped the side of his face and moaned. The red object fell on the ground and rolled away—I glanced through the dense underbrush to see the bandit who threw the pomegranate. I heard someone scampering through the scrub but gave up on the idea of chasing him—I'd never catch him.

Simon had knelt down with his nubby fingers covering the wound, fingers worn away from the living death that would eventually kill him. I rushed over and crouched beside him. "Are you all right?"

He nodded but refused to look at me—horrified that I was so close to him.

I glanced at the father and son who stood a few feet away. The father approached, but I could tell he was hesitant.

The young boy looked up at his father. "I tell Mommy Daniel brought us food." He ran back inside the cave.

I stepped back from Simon, wishing I could do more, but my presence was painfully a hindrance. I watched as the boy's father tended to the injured man. Simon stood after a minute and seemed to be okay, though rather shaken.

"Thank you," he said to me.

I nodded.

The two of them picked up the supplies and hauled them inside the cave.

I'd promised I would be more caring. I didn't know the cost—until now.

CHAPTER 9 UNSPOKEN GIFTS

I sat in the lobby with Dr. Luke and Ami. Ami's brother, Levi, joined us later. Most of the patrons had finished eating. Levi set his walking stick underneath the table and stretched out in the chair beside us.

The women had cleared the tables and the rattling of dishes filtered in from the back room. The men lingered after the meal, catching up on the news from Rome and Jerusalem. Conversation the night before had centered on the Roman soldier who had tried to seize me. My story and the death of the disabled man had made the rounds. I would have preferred anonymity.

Ami was one of Dr. Luke's patients even though he had no obvious physical ailments, but he had epilepsy. Dr. Luke and others had tried for years to heal him. He'd have made a good lawyer but his illness prevented that.

Ami was animated tonight, more than I had seen him before. He stood and walked around the room, tapping each table to get people's attention. "Wake up, now is not the time to sleep." Most of the men appeared bored, but not ready to retire for the evening.

I took my cue from Dr. Luke who listened attentively.

Ami began his comments, "I had heard so much about Yochanan the Immerser that I had to see for myself. I went down to the Jordan River today."

Dr. Luke raised his eyebrow.

Ami continued, "A large crowd came to hear Yochanan and many asked to be cleansed from their sins. He dunked several in the river."

Ami paced back and forth, as he spoke. "The man was dressed in camel's hair with a leather belt around his waist. 'Turn from

47

your sins, return to God,' he said. Ami raised his hand as if in imitation. 'The Kingdom of Heaven is near.' The common folk were drawn to him. Some are even calling him a prophet."

Several men shifted in their seat. I couldn't tell if they were interested or bored.

Ami asked the question many were already asking. "Who do you say Yochanan the Immerser is?"

No one dared to speak.

Ami continued. "Some temple leaders showed up, priests and Levites."

When he said this, the tension in the room increased a few decibels. Historically, I knew Yochanan to be nothing more than an oddity who lived in the wilderness, though Christians considered him a great man. I was more interested in the temple, the center of worship before its destruction in 70 A.D. The Muslims built the Dome of the Rock many years later over the temple base. I tried to imagine what the temple looked like.

Levi, Ami's brother, whispered, bringing me back to reality. "If he keeps going with this, we're going to have a firestorm."

Ami continued. "The priests wanted to ask Yochanan some questions. I didn't know the men, but they were sent by the Levites. Yochanan treated them very disrespectfully."

"Such as?" one man asked.

"He called the Pharisees and the Sadducees a brood of vipers."

A murmur stirred in the room.

"That probably went over well," one man scoffed.

"He told the religious leaders to return to God," Ami said. "If that isn't an insult, I don't know what is. That's like telling a doctor he needs to go back to medical school."

A man behind me spoke up. "We haven't had a prophet in 450 years, since Malachi. Maybe he is the next great one."

Ami pointed to him. "But if he were a prophet, why would he tell them to repent and turn to God? These are very learned, religious men."

Dr. Luke said, "The prophets were always critical of the rulers and the priests, and most were martyred because of it."

Ami turned to the doctor. "So you say he is a prophet?"

Dr. Luke shrugged. "Time will reveal if he is a true prophet."

48

Ami focused on me. "Daniel, you're from Jerusalem. What have you heard about this supposed prophet? Who do you say he is?"

I shook my head. "I don't know."

"You don't know?" repeated Ami. "Daniel, everyone in Jerusalem is aware of Yochanan the Immerser."

The tension rose in the room. I needed to come up with something to say that would be neutral.

Ami pointed his finger at me. "What are you hiding, Daniel, son of Aviv? You show up here from Jerusalem and seem ignorant, yet I know you are a smart lad. Surely you must know about Yochanan the Immerser."

"Maybe he is one of their followers," someone said.

I shook my head. "No, I'm not one of his followers. He'll be beheaded because of his impertinence."

"Beheaded?" Ami repeated. He seemed surprised by my prediction.

I had said too much. For good or worse, that was all I remembered about John the Baptist, as he was commonly known in Christian circles. Jews who did consider him a historical person called him a false prophet. I didn't want to say that for fear someone in the room might be a secret follower.

Another man commented, "He attacks everyone, including King Herod Antipas."

"King Herod is a wicked king," Levi said.

The conversation turned away from me and the discussion went elsewhere. As I sat listening, I became aware of a stranger outside. I reached over and tapped Dr. Luke on the shoulder. "A man needs your help outside."

"What did you say, Daniel?"

I repeated myself, this time drawing too much attention.

"A person is at the door," Levi said. "Check outside. Daniel says he heard someone."

Ami paused as a hotel guest went to the front door.

Shuffling noises emanated from the entrance. "Tell Doctor Luke to come. A man has been beaten and is bleeding."

Dr. Luke stared at me. I didn't know what to say. How did I know?

CHAPTER 10 DISCOVERY

T wo Weeks Later

I no longer feared for my life, but I did fear never finding my way home. After all, I had no idea how I had arrived in first century Israel—which seemed barbaric. What would it be like to live here for the rest of my life? I would never see my sister again, or my brother. Jacob couldn't reveal his whereabouts except to one family member—or my mother. I chuckled. I would probably miss my mother the least. Then there were my friends. I sighed. No more computers, Internet, movies or cars—how would I survive?

I touched the ridge on my forehead—the only visible link to my past besides my contacts. The healed mark reminded me that something had cut me. Reflections from fine glass showed a jagged mark that would probably never go away.

Without readily available pen and paper as in modern times, I was forced to make a mental checklist of what we needed. Dr. Luke would tell me what to get, and I'd learned to match those things with associations that I wouldn't forget. I found this a little challenging at first, but with practice, it came quite naturally.

It wouldn't take me long to buy the supplies and then I could enjoy a leisurely walk through town. The bazaar was similar to Jerusalem's Old City. Dothan was a major hub along the well-traveled route between Samaria and Nazareth—a good thing since we received most of our news from weary travelers passing through.

As I walked past a women's boutique I began to daydream. What if I found a young girl I liked—would I want to stay? I shrugged. Women's stores were not called boutiques in the first century. While I was Jewish, I felt like an outsider. The nuances of language and customs in the first century were frustrating. How would any Jewish girl here find me attractive? I hoped I didn't appear as awkward to others as I sometimes felt.

Someone called my name, "Daniel."

I looked around. No, it couldn't be! Was that my sister behind the counter? I rushed over to see.

"What are you doing here?" Martha asked. "Mother said you wanted to finish your studies before you came to see my new store."

I stared at her. Was she really my sister? She looked like her, she knew my name, and she had my sister's mannerisms, but what was she doing here?

Martha leaned towards me with concern on her face—"Daniel, are you all right?"

I chuckled. "I'm fine. I—I just didn't expect to see you."

She threw up her hands. "Why else would you be in Dothan but to see me?"

I smiled. I needed to embrace her reality. "Yes, I decided to come." I remembered all the pranks I had played on her when we were young. I had been cruel at her expense, but fortunately, she never held it against me. Did she travel back in time, too? No—my sister in 2015 hadn't opened a store in Dothan. This was a different reality. I told myself, things were not as they appeared.

I stepped back to admire her business and waved my hand. "Is this all yours?"

"Yes," she exclaimed. "Let me show you around."

The shop was small, but for a woman to own her own store in any century was remarkable. I had a new appreciation for my sister's talents. She inherited our father's business sense.

Too many questions went through my head. I would start with the easy ones first. "So how do you get these fine linens from Syria?"

"Traders are always willing to do business with me, so I have been able to avoid the journey myself. Our father's name is good among the Arabs," she added.

Sadness hit me that he was no longer with us. She sensed my feelings.

"Don't be upset," said Martha. "We are doing what Father would have wanted us to do—pursuing our passions, even though it took a while to convince Mother to let us choose."

So was my mother here too? Was Mother the same in both places—in Jerusalem during the first century as well as 2015?

If only I could remember what happened after I saw the bright light. Had one of our enemies invented technology that could send a person back in time? Or maybe they had brainwashed Martha—no, there was no way they could create something this elaborate.

"Daniel, are you listening to me?" Martha asked.

I turned my attention back to her. "Sorry," I said. "Daydreaming."

"Anyway," Martha continued, "the Silk Road gives me great exposure here—less competition and more business than in Jerusalem."

I nodded. "A good business decision on your part."

I tried to listen to her, but my thoughts were on time travel. How did I travel back in time? I thought about Einstein's Theory of Relativity. The only problem was his theory dealt with traveling forwards in time, not backwards. So how did I go backwards?

Martha waved her hand in front of my face. "Daniel, are you listening to me?"

"Yes, yes, I am. Sorry."

She talked about the price of imported cloths, but I didn't recognize the brands. My mind strayed. Why the first century? Why couldn't I have visited the Renaissance period when Mozart and Handel wrote classical music? Or why couldn't I have spent an afternoon in Florence with Leonardo Da Vinci? I would have told him that many of his drawings would become a reality hundreds of years later and he wasn't a bastard son because of his illegitimacy.

What about the early 1900s? I could have met Albert Einstein. Why, God, this place and this time period?

"Daniel, you aren't listening to me again," Martha chided.

"I am," I assured her.

"What did I say?"

"You were talking about the price of various imported cloths."

Martha smiled. "You were listening." She added, "You never were much into the family business, were you?"

I shook my head. "I don't have the enthusiasm for it that you and Father had."

Martha reached over and laid her hand on mine. "Daniel, be well. You have other gifts. God is good."

I laughed. Martha in 2015 was probably the most religious of any of us. Perhaps this Martha was a twin to my sister. She seemed to have no knowledge of anything except the present. She talked about our mother and missing father.

Did another Daniel, son of Aviv, live in first century Jerusalem? I'd heard that everyone has a twin. Maybe my twin lived here. What would happen if I went to Jerusalem and met him—or me? I was envious that apparently my twin was able to pursue being a doctor while I was stuck in the wrong century.

"Would you like some water?" Martha asked.

"Sure," I replied. "That would be great."

She stepped over to the water jug and filled my mug. Perhaps God was trying to get my attention. I had abandoned my Jewish heritage for too long.

I shrugged. "Ani lo mevin," I said under my breath. I didn't understand how it happened, but I was overjoyed to meet Martha. She seemed happy to be running her own store. Was she really my sister, though? What could I ask her that only she would know?

She handed me the cup and I took several sips before testing her.

"Martha, have you heard any news recently from our brother, Jacob?"

Martha frowned. "You know I can't talk about Jacob."

I shrugged. "I'll be glad when this mission is over."

Martha nodded. "Soon it will be."

She was definitely my sister.

CHAPTER II OPPORTUNITY

I arrived back at Jacob's Inn encouraged. Maybe there were others like me. How else could people come up with such crazy plots in movies and books? And those that couldn't learn to function—maybe they were the ones who ended up at treatment centers. This much I was sure of—I'd be the same person if I was born in the first century as I was in the twenty-first century

As I unpacked the supplies and put them away, Dr. Luke entered the lobby. He walked over and watched me, not saying anything at first.

The doctor was dressed in his usual white robe and sandals, the typical clothing worn around here, but I imagined him wearing a white coat in a prestigious hospital.

He approached me and placed his hand on my shoulder. "Daniel, you're a hard worker."

"Thank you."

I continued to stock the shelves as my spirits soared at the unexpected compliment.

"I have something I want to share with you, an opportunity," Dr. Luke said.

I stopped and looked up.

The doctor had a big grin on his face. "Can we talk about something important?"

I nodded. When people say such things, I think I'm in trouble, so I was glad he began with the compliment.

I followed him over to the window table. A gentle breeze from the north blew in making the room airy and comfortable. The window overlooked a small garden that butted up next to the road. A street merchant by the entrance to the portico was selling fresh fruit and cakes to some weary travelers.

Dr. Luke's voice brought me back inside the room and I listened closely.

"Daniel, I appreciate your help with the lepers and the patients. You've made many friends here."

I'd never felt myself half as caring as Dr. Luke. "You set a good example, Doctor Luke. Someday I hope to go to medical school."

He grinned. "You'd make an excellent doctor. When that time comes, and I don't think it's that far into the future, I'd be glad to write a recommendation for you."

"That would be great." I was glad someone thought I could make it through medical school.

He leaned towards me. "You know Theophilus is a good friend of mine."

"Yes, Doctor Luke." I had heard the name mentioned a few times. The man was very wealthy and a high-ranking official in the Roman government.

Dr. Luke leaned back with his hands behind his head. "Theophilus and I grew up in Antioch and attended school together when we were young. He chose to study law and I went into medicine."

"Both great professions," I commented.

"Yes, indeed. Our friendship has continued despite the heavy hand of the Romans on the Jews and his political involvement in Roman affairs." He laughed. "Many times we have different leanings, but it makes for great conversation when we have those rare visits together."

I smiled in agreement.

Dr. Luke continued. "I was in Caesarea yesterday, and Theo mentioned that a man who works for him, a scribe skilled in languages, has a mute son whom he loves. The lad is getting older and his nanny feels that he needs—well, a respectable young man to guide him through the teenage years. You know what I mean?"

"Yes."

"But he can't talk and frustrates the nanny, so much so that the father thought having a young man to mentor the boy when he's out of town would be of great help."

I agreed. "I'm sure it would be."

"Brutus, son of Dirk, would pay very well, provide room and board, and you could put that money towards your education."

"Do they live in Dothan?"

"No, they live in Nazareth, but it's close enough you could come by and visit from time to time—I hope."

"Sure."

Dr. Luke handed me a parchment with the details. "Here is a map that shows where they live."

I read the note. "So the young boy's name is Nathan and he's twelve?"

Dr. Luke nodded. "That's all I know. I've never met him or Brutus, but Theo spoke highly of the family. Brutus is Theo's administrator in Caesarea. With Palestine being the bridge between the North and the South, he's an asset for peaceful relations among the Romans, the Jews, the Samaritans, and everyone else."

"He must also be pretty smart, too." Foreign languages were not my strength in school.

Dr. Luke nodded. "He asked if I knew of anyone that would be a strong candidate. That's when I thought of you, though I hate to lose you."

Dr. Luke reminisced wistfully before continuing. "He also said if the new hire could manage the livestock when the current farmhand couldn't, he would reward him with bonus pay."

"I think I could learn easily enough, Doctor Luke."

"Great. I will send word to my friend that you will come as soon as possible. If you ever travel to Caesarea, you must stop by and meet him."

Dr. Luke and I stood and shook hands. I hated leaving Dothan, but I sensed this would be a great opportunity.

Dr. Luke added as we walked outside, "You know, Daniel, you are able to perceive the needs of people in uncanny ways, almost as if you can read people's minds. I see that as a gift from

SEVENTH DIMENSION – THE KING BOOK 2

God. For a mute boy, that would be a miracle, to know what his needs are without being able to say them."

"I never looked at it like that, as being a gift from God."

"Just a thought," Dr. Luke said. "And a great asset for someone who wants to study medicine."

I reflected on Dr. Luke's words. I saw mind reading as a skill I had developed. The more I focused on people's needs, the more I was able to perceive those needs, like learning to play the guitar. The more time I practiced, the better I played.

But that it came from God—until now I'd thought God was angry with me. I had refused to go to the synagogue since my father disappeared and had long given up praying. Why would God want to give me anything?

My musings turned to Nazareth. I hadn't been to the town in years—many unresolved issues made it a difficult place to live.

CHAPTER 12 THE BEGGAR

I left the next morning to travel to Galilee. I had said goodbye to everyone the night before, promising to come back and visit when I had the first opportunity.

As I passed the leper colony, I thought about stopping. I had not had a conversation with them since that first encounter, but they were never far from my mind—especially the little boy who didn't have leprosy but lived with his leprous mom and dad.

If I wanted to arrive in Nazareth by sundown, however, I shouldn't stop. My focus shifted to the road ahead, the caravan route for traders—and one of the most ancient highways in the world. Too many wars depended on this highway—Hammurabi of Babylon, Sargon I of Agade, Thutmose III of Egypt, and more recently, the Crusaders and Alexander the Great. I shuddered at Israel's long and violent history.

The rolling hills flattened into long valleys dotted with rocky outcroppings surrounded by cedar, cypress and olive trees. I expected to run into roadblocks or checkpoints but Jews lived peacefully here with other tribes, unlike modern times.

What happened to cause the animosity? I kicked the rocks under my sandals, frustrated that things were the way they were. What if we could go back and change the future?

A young shepherd boy stood guard in a nearby fertile field. He was no more than ten or eleven. He was watching over his family's most prized possession. His long stick was all he needed to keep away predators. The lad would probably never attend school or leave the country. His dreams began and ended on this small strip of land that had been in his family for generations.

Opportunity to become more than a shepherd would never cross his mind. He waved as I walked by. I smiled and waved back. Maybe his way of life was better—simple and predictable. An honest lifestyle that was good enough for David—until God chose him to be king.

The sun parked overhead making me sweat. I lamented that I had to walk rather than ride in a comfortable, air-conditioned car that would only require a fraction of the time to get there. Maybe I could muster enough strength to travel a little further before stopping to rest. As I came to the plain of Megiddo, I was surprised at how little the area had changed.

From my high school history, I knew over two hundred battles had been fought here. Struggle to control the area was legendary. An elaborate mythology about Megiddo and stories of prophecy had survived through the centuries. Many so-called prophets predicted a cataclysmic battle to take place here in the future.

Israel had had so many skirmishes recently that fatalists feared World War III was imminent. Armageddon was never far from the minds of many.

I stopped to eat on the mountain of Megiddo. The panoramic view was spectacular. I admired the lush green valley—the most productive agricultural area in Israel. I dug into my bag and set out my water. I ate some figs and nuts and soaked in the afternoon sun.

Then I heard a noise and looked behind me. I suspected an animal had crept up, looking for an easy meal from my scraps. I was surprised to see an old woman.

She approached me as if she knew me. The strange woman wore a green dress and carried a brown bag over her shoulder. She was bald except for a few wispy strands of hair. Her sunken cheeks, boney forehead, and bulging eyes reminded me of someone you might see in a graveyard. Her stringy fingers clasped her bag. I wanted to stand but my legs felt as if they had turned to jelly.

"Can I have some of your food?" she asked. She moved closer to me. Maybe she was a homeless beggar.

"Here." I gave her the rest of my meal hoping she would go away. I didn't want to share my water. I needed that. I scooted back so she wasn't as close. She had an unpleasant odor that was familiar to me, but I couldn't place it.

She gobbled up the food as if she were famished. She didn't say anything until she finished it.

"How is your journey?" she asked.

"Fine." She made me feel uneasy.

"Where are you headed?"

"To Capernaum," I lied.

"Where are you from?"

I didn't like being interrogated. This time I didn't answer.

She turned and looked across the plains.

I followed her eyes.

A red horse carrying a dark rider galloped across the field. The rider wielded a sword and I perceived he was slashing objects, though whatever he was striking was invisible.

"You are that rider," she said.

"What?" I asked.

She smiled and revealed several missing front teeth. "I'm your benefactor."

I shook my head. "No, you can't be my benefactor."

"Danger lurks in Galilee," she said.

I stared at her. I told her I was going to Capernaum.

She quit smiling and pointed her bony finger at me. "Things are not as they appear."

I moved away from the woman and glanced back at the horse but the rider was gone. The horse galloped further and further away.

"Your fate," she said, "if you go to Galilee." The strange woman-turned-diviner walked away. When she was gone, I bent over the ledge and heaved up my lunch. What little I ate.

I tried to calm myself. Was she the one who paid for my motel room? How did she know I was going to Galilee and not Capernaum?

"Shoot," I said, "it'd be just my luck to have her for a benefactor, an old panhandler who looked like the devil."

I picked up my belongings and took off, no longer excited about going to Galilee. Was I about to do something I would later regret? I looked back to make sure she wasn't following me— whoever or whatever she was. I hoped I never saw her again.

CHAPTER 13 RANDOMNESS

I couldn't put the beggar woman out of my mind and kept thinking about her strange words, "Things are not as they appear." How could she pretend to know my fate? Only God knows those things and I couldn't imagine him sharing my future with someone who appeared to be a freeloader. I shook my head as if I could shake reality back the way it belonged.

My mind wandered. Maybe life at its simplest came down to nothing more than choices—except I didn't choose to come to first century Palestine.

What if our future wasn't predetermined and we could choose? Suppose God put us into situations we didn't like to test us? Attempting to remove God from my life had made me powerless. I thought it would be the opposite—empower me. Without God, was life nothing more than a series of random events? I couldn't change the past, but what about the future? Did God just program me like a robot or did he give me free will? What was the point of living if we were no more than robots?

Maybe more than one reality existed at the same time and something caused them to collide into one reality. What would happen if the two got mixed up?

I kicked some rocks in my path. Dr. Luke had provided a sense of security. Whom would I rely on now? Would I listen to an old demented woman—who claimed to know more about my future than I did?

I remembered Psalm 23 from the Tanakh. "Though I walk through the valley of the shadow of death, I will fear no evil. Thy rod and thy staff, they comfort me."

The sheep did not fear its enemies because the shepherd protected them, like the young lad I had witnessed. The boy relied on a cane and his faith in God to keep away the wolves.

Why hadn't God protected my father? Why did he bring me to this strange fate?

I pressed ahead. Speaking of choices—which road should I take? If I went west, I'd drown in the ocean. If I went east, I'd venture into enemy territory. If I went south, I'd be back at the inn. If I went north, a young boy unable to speak for himself needed me to speak for him. I clung to that. I swiped my forehead with my arm, as if I could wipe away the fear.

Suddenly, a crow out of nowhere sky-bombed me. I swatted at him, "Go away you buzzard." The black bird squawked and took off. That was too deliberate—he meant to attack me.

I sped up, more anxious than ever to get to Brutus's house. Nervous energy propelled me to run.

I soon arrived at the outskirts of Lower Galilee on the northern ridge of the Jezreel Valley. I studied the map. My destination was close.

I paused to survey my surroundings. I was surprised at how desolate the town was. Besides the olive groves, nothing else seemed familiar. In 2015, thousands of Arabs and Jewish residents pressed in on each other, living in crowded communities side by side. In the first century, the small community eked out a quiet existence. Its notoriety was linked to a man Christians called Yeshua—or Jesus. Culture shock at the difference between the first century and 2015 made me feel like I had traveled a long way from home. I had in a strange sort of way—two thousand years into my past.

I remembered Ami's comments about the Immerser. I shuddered. Christians called him John the Baptist. It wasn't long after the Immerser's clashes with the Jewish authorities that the man from Nazareth came on the scene. I sighed. Why did I have to come to the area where he lived? Maybe that was why the old woman told me to go back.

Of course, until the Immerser's beheading, the rabbi wouldn't have much influence. I hoped that was years away. I wished I had read some of that book Lilly had given me. I regretted my mocking attitude—I could have learned something if I hadn't been so close-minded.

I walked a couple more hours and reached the man's house. The structure sat nestled beneath a cliff surrounded by a lush green pasture. For a Gentile, Brutus had done quite well. Rome paid administrators nicely and didn't tax the Gentiles as they did the Jews. Now that the moment had arrived, I was excited. I walked up to the door and knocked.

A few seconds later, a burly man greeted me. He was fit and trim for his advancing years. His aging eyes were gentle and his complexion darker than I expected.

I introduced myself. "I'm Daniel, son of Aviv, and I'm here to see Brutus, son of Dirk."

"Daniel, come in, come in. I'm Brutus, son of Dirk—call me Brutus, please—welcome. I'm so glad to meet you."

After our initial introductions, he closed the door and motioned me to sit. "Please, make yourself comfortable."

I did and glanced around the exquisitely furnished room. Brutus had a broad taste in cultures from his travels and exposure to many languages.

Soon a woman walked in half her husband's age. I was surprised at the difference in demeanor between the two. She eyed me with skepticism, without warmth. Her eyes roamed my body, making me feel uncomfortable.

"Let me introduce you to my wonderful wife. This is Scylla."

"I'm honored to meet you," I said.

"Welcome—"

"Daniel, son of Aviv," I said.

—"Daniel, son of Aviv," she repeated.

Scylla reminded me of an aging beauty queen. Her long face appeared drawn and her pale eyes had lost the glimmer of yesteryear. Her husband deserved better, but I chided myself for being so judgmental.

Soon a boy who looked to be about twelve entered the room. His mannerisms reminded me of an immature child. He avoided eye contact and walked clumsily. He looked away without saying anything. I sensed anger mixed with distrust. I would have to earn his acceptance.

"Nathan," said Brutus, "meet Daniel, son of Aviv."

The boy finally made eye contact before turning away. I smiled hoping to crack through his steel façade. He didn't know I could reach beyond it—yet.

An tense moment followed when no one said anything. Suddenly the boy cried out, followed by a full-blown tantrum. Smiles left everyone's faces and introductions were over. I sat and watched, not sure what to do.

Nathan thrashed about, rubbing his feet across the wooden floor and flailing his hands.

Brutus spoke gently, "Stop. I'm here." He grabbed the boy underneath his arms and pulled him over into his lap. Brutus then held him until Nathan quit struggling and became quiet, rocking him back and forth.

I tried to read his thoughts. Confusion and fear filled his mind.

"Tell Nathan that I'm not going to take him away."

Brutus did as I instructed and the boy seemed to relax.

"Nathan needs time. Tell him I'm his friend and I will live here for a little while."

The boy's father did again as I instructed, and calmness settled over Nathan's demeanor. He eyed me now with less apprehension.

Brutus nodded. "I think this will work."

I smiled.

A young woman carrying bags of food entered through the front door. She was tall and slender, with long, dark brown hair. She brought to mind my sister, Martha. The girl did not seem to notice me.

"Come over here, Mari, and meet Daniel, son of Aviv."

When Brutus said my name, she turned white.

Brutus perceived something was wrong and lifted Nathan from his lap to catch her, but she instantly regained her composure. If she existed in my own time, I would know her—pretty young women never escaped my attention.

66

I stood. "Nice to meet you, Mari."

A moment later Scylla clapped her hands. "We've had too much drama. Let's lighten things up a bit. Mari, please prepare some food for our guest. I'll be in my quarters."

The two women ambled towards the back. I scooted closer to Nathan. I soon realized nothing was ever as easy as it first appeared. The real work had just begun. I would earn every shekel I made, especially when I met Judd, the caretaker of the animals.

CHAPTER 14 SECRETS

My first test as a "big brother" occurred a couple of weeks after my arrival. Brutus was on leave from his duties in Jerusalem to help with my transition to the household, but Roman officials showed up early one morning. They claimed Brutus must go with them to Jerusalem. It was difficult for Brutus to conduct business from Nazareth. Because he loved the Galilean countryside, he endured the long trips to Jerusalem and Caesarea from Nazareth.

When I heard Brutus was leaving, I wanted Judd to show me how to prepare Brutus's horse for travel. I went back to the cave and found him.

Judd laughed. "Don't you know anything about horses?"

I shrugged. "I just want to see how Brutus likes his horse saddled. That way, when you go on vacation, I can do it for you. Or if you are busy with other duties."

Judd became less defensive. "Well, then. Grab that saddle with the horns."

"Horns?" I repeated.

"Yeah. Hanging on the wall."

I looked for a horned saddle, whatever that was. "This one?"

"No, that one," Judd said impatiently.

"This?"

"No, the one to the left of that one."

Why had I volunteered to help? I grabbed the one with four horns and carried it over to him. Judd put the saddle on the animal's back.

69

"What about the stirrups?"

Judd scrunched his nose. "Stirrups?"

"Yeah, for the feet."

"Never heard of that," Judd said.

"Oh." Maybe they didn't use stirrups in first century Palestine. I couldn't imagine riding a horse without stirrups.

Soon Judd had the horse ready. I attempted some small talk. "How long have you been working here?"

Judd laughed. "Our families go back generations. We are probably related."

"That's interesting."

"Lots of history you don't want to know," he added. "Don't be nosy."

I threw up my hands. "Just making conversation." Family secrets he didn't want to share—at least not with me.

Judd added, "Whatever you do in this cave, don't mess with Assassin."

"Assassin?" I repeated.

"My donkey." He pointed to a large red-haired brute.

The animal appeared so mean-tempered I didn't know why he thought I would want to touch his animal anyway.

A few hours after Brutus left, things went awry. I heard Nathan's cries and ran up to his room. The timing was unfortunate because Mari was usually around to help, but she had taken the day off to visit a friend.

When I entered, I saw Scylla slapping Nathan's face. "Stop it, you stupid child," she screamed at him.

I rushed over to intervene. "Don't slap him," I said. "Let me help."

She stepped back, surprised at my sudden appearance. I'd heard his cries before they were audible. No one knew about my special gift. I had caught her doing something that Brutus would never approve of. How often had she done that? I wrapped my arms around the young lad.

"Nathan, I'm here." His pain could not be spoken. Now I could be his voice. I gave him hope.

Scylla walked towards the door. "Thank you for coming. Things are not as they appear." She slammed the door behind her.

When would things ever be as they appear? I rocked Nathan to soothe his cries. The boy probably had reason to be frightened when his father left.

I took Nathan outside and we spent the afternoon in the pasture with the sheep. Perhaps being around the timid animals would do him good. Soon he forgot about the incident as his thoughts went elsewhere, particularly when we came across a snake. He pointed at it excitedly and I could hear him say through mental telepathy, "It's not poisonous."

'How do you know?" I asked.

"I know all the snakes around here," he said through unspoken words.

I was impressed. I didn't know much about snakes, except for the Palestinian viper, the most common poisonous one, and I didn't know if it was around in the first century. I suppose when you can't speak, you find ways to occupy your time, especially when you feel isolated and alone.

I noticed Judd watching from a distance, as if noting everything I did. I shook off the distraction and became preoccupied with Nathan. Our laughter lifted his dampened spirits. Perhaps someday a miracle might loosen his tongue.

CHAPTER I5 ATTACK

F ive months later

Brutus's trips had become more frequent because of unrest in the country. Yochanan the Immerser had stirred things up, though I hadn't heard word of his beheading. I had even heard Yeshua mentioned in passing on the streets. I knew the firestorm that was about to be unleashed.

I sighed. I couldn't have been brought to a more controversial place than Galilee in the first century. If God existed, and I believed he did, why did he bring me here? I was a non-practicing Jew who wanted nothing to do with Yeshua of Nazareth. Why hadn't God found a Christian to bring here? Why me?

The days turned into weeks. I had not been back to Dothan but fondly remembered Dr. Luke, thankful he had found me this job. Brutus paid well and my money was growing. I kept it hidden in my room.

One afternoon I was repairing the leg of a chair in the dining area. I considered taking it to the local carpenter, but I didn't think the chair was fancy enough to warrant the expense.

Brutus was somewhere else and Mari had gone into town. Nathan was taking a nap. The house was quiet. I was on my knees finishing up when what I perceived to be fingers caressed my neck. I reached behind me and felt a hand.

I stood and turned to face her. Scylla's eyes were drunk with wine. She threw herself at me.

"No," I said.

I tried to extricate myself from her embrace.

Scylla persisted, running her fingers through my hair. "Oh, Daniel, my love—the signs in the heavens are there, like when Brutus came to me to read his future."

I looked away so she couldn't kiss me. "What signs?"

She burned with unbridled passion. "I have powers you don't know about."

I fell backwards tripping over the chair that I had just fixed. The noise echoed in the room, loud enough to wake Nathan.

When I stood and tried to escape, she trapped me against the wall. She whispered into my ear. "How do you think I got Brutus to marry me?"

"I—I don't know."

Suddenly she clawed my neck and cried out in a haunting voice. I writhed as she ran back into her private quarters. When I touched the open wound, blood tinged my fingers. I looked up and saw Judd standing in the doorway. A knowing smirk covered his face.

"It's not what you think," I said.

"I can keep secrets." He rolled his eyes and walked away.

Did he believe I had attacked her? What if she made false accusations to her husband? She had a witness who wouldn't mind ruining me. I stared at the broken chair. I should have taken it to the carpenter.

CHAPTER 16 ANNOUNCEMENT

I was always thankful when Brutus came home as his good-natured humor lifted everyone's spirits. He had a proclivity for speaking in multiple languages at once, and would wink when we gave him a blank stare. This time he returned more excited than usual and sought us out individually.

"I have a big announcement to make," he said several times during the day. "Join me tonight at dinner. We'll celebrate with a big pot of red meat and vegetables."

I spent the day pondering what the big announcement might be.

The aroma of salt, onions, garlic, and cumin soon filled the house. At last, when mealtime came, we were all seated, waiting to hear the big news.

Brutus asked me to say a blessing and I spoke a Hebrew prayer.

"Let everyone get their food first," Brutus said.

We took turns as each person took a plate full. Red meat for dinner was a rarity.

At last, Brutus raised his wine glass. "Let's toast."

We all held up our glasses.

He smiled and made eye contact with each of us before the big announcement. "Shale, my daughter, is coming for a visit."

I didn't know he had a daughter. Who else knew?

Scylla's smile left her face but returned before anyone else noticed.

Judd showed no emotion, but his lack of joy seemed strange. He set down his drink and stared at his plate.

Nathan sat up straighter and his eyes bulged.

Mari took a sip of the wine.

Scylla spoke first. "When? You should have told me earlier. We need to prepare her room, make everything ready."

"We have two days," Brutus said.

"So you talked with her mother?" Scylla asked.

Brutus wiped his mouth, set down his napkin, and leaned back in his chair. "Her mother asked if she could come. She's fourteen now, a young woman." Brutus lifted his eyebrow and glanced at Judd.

What did Judd have to do with this? I couldn't read minds well enough to know specific details except with Nathan. I could only read feelings.

The room was quiet.

Judd had eaten only half his food. "May I be excused?" he asked.

His request was ignored.

Mari seemed oblivious to Judd's sudden lack of appetite. "I look forward to meeting her. We'll do everything we can to make her stay comfortable. Do you know her preferences for food?"

Brutus puckered his lips. "I haven't seen her since she was a baby."

I wanted to keep the conversation going. "This must be a big event for you to meet her."

"Yes. I'm very excited."

"Let me know if I can do anything to help."

"Thank you, Daniel. Make sure Nathan is on his good behavior. You know, I never told him he had a sister. I should have."

Nathan smiled broadly.

I glanced at Nathan. "I have a feeling this will be good for him, to meet his sibling."

After dinner, I plodded to my room thinking about Brutus's daughter. What did she look like? What prompted her visit? How long would she stay?

The next day I helped Judd with cleaning the stalls and the cave. Scylla said Shale would be coming on a donkey that belonged to the family. Brutus had loaned the donkey to a friend a few months earlier. Brutus had asked the man to send the donkey ahead to fetch her.

Judd was glad for my help, though his aloofness bothered me.

I enjoyed being around the animals almost as much as I liked being with Nathan, but I left Judd's prize donkey, Assassin, alone.

The day before Shale's arrival, we received another strange visitor. A small brown and white dog arrived on the back portico. She walked around the outside of the house, sniffing in the corners and checking out the new herb garden I'd planted. I shooed her away before she destroyed the plants.

She ran over to the gate and started digging. A little mound of dirt gathered behind her legs and she stuck her nose in the hole. The four-legged animal emerged with a large bone. I laughed. When had she buried that thing?

After digging out the bone, she brought it to me and laid it at my feet. I knelt down and scratched her behind the ear. She barked and ran over to the entrance to the cave.

When Judd came out, she scurried inside.

"Do you know that dog?" I asked. I was concerned about what havoc she might cause and followed her into the cave.

"Much-Afraid, did she come back?"

I pointed to where she had left her bone. "Yeah, I guess. I mean, she just arrived and dug up her bone."

I added, "What a strange name for a dog."

Judd shrugged. "Much-Afraid ran away after Brutus loaned his friend the donkey. I heard she showed up at the friend's farm and stayed. Now that Baruch is coming back, I guess she decided to return."

Judd stepped back inside the cave and walked over to the water bin to wash his hands. His sudden obsession with hand washing seemed odd. He had also taken to mumbling.

What did you say?" I asked.

His eyes darted back and forth. "Nothing important."

Whatever was bothering him, he didn't want to talk about it. I wandered outside and retrieved Much-Afraid's bone and then went back inside the cave. I'd give it to her later.

The dog appeared to visit all the animals but hung around one pig in particular. The canine dug herself a bed in the cool dirt beside the stall. As the dog crouched in front of the pig's gate, the squealing hog lumbered over to the entrance. If I didn't know any better, I'd say they were old friends getting reacquainted.

Her resemblance to the dog that followed me around in the old city of Jerusalem was remarkable. Was it a coincidence?

That evening I lay in the grassy field staring up at the beet red sky. I had been here five months, but it didn't feel as if so much time had passed.

Much-Afraid approached wagging her tail. She licked my hand and curled up beside me. I remembered her bone and pulled it out of my bag. She chewed contentedly as I scratched her head.

My thoughts returned to Brutus's daughter. I liked the sound of the name, Shale, but I had a feeling someone else did too—even if he refused to talk about it.

CHAPTER 17 HOUSE GUEST

E vening turned into night. What secrets hid among the stars? The wings of light covered the blackness creating unbelievable beauty. I sighed. How could I admire God's handiwork and still refuse to worship him?

I relented. "I know you are the God of Isaac, Jacob and Abraham, but when are you going to be mindful of me?" Clouds covered the moon creating make-believe shadows.

Did God make deals with man? I didn't know. I wanted to believe he still cared.

The next morning I rose early and finished my chores. Homeschooling Nathan took up a good portion of the day. I'd read to him in Greek and Latin. The chance to expand his mind would help him in other ways even if he never said a word, and I enjoyed the chance to hone my Greek skills.

Brutus had scrolls in languages from all over the world, including Egyptian and Arabic. We spoke Aramaic most of the time. I was fortunate that my father spoke Aramaic having grown up in Malula, Syria, where Aramaic was common. How else could I have spoken the language of the people in the first century?

When I returned the Greek and Latin scrolls following our language studies, I saw a Hebrew scroll I had never noticed before. Curious, I pulled it out.

It was from the book of Isaiah. I glanced at a passage where someone had made some illegible notes.

"He had no form or beauty, that we should look at him:
No charm, that we should find him pleasing.
He was despised, shunned by men
A man of suffering, familiar with disease.
As one who hid his face from us,
He was despised, we held him of no account.
Yet it was our sickness that he was bearing,
Our suffering that he endured.
We accounted him plagued,
Smitten and afflicted by God;
But he was wounded because of our sins,
Crushed because of our iniquities.
He bore the chastisement that made us whole,
And by his bruises we were healed."

I paused to consider the words. Of whom was Isaiah speaking? I didn't remember reading these verses in the Tanakh—but when was the last time I had even opened the Scriptures?

I read a little more.

"He was maltreated, yet he was submissive,
He did not open his mouth;
Like a sheep being led to slaughter,
Like a ewe, dumb before those who shear her,
He did not open his mouth.
By oppressive judgment he was taken away,
Who could describe his abode?
For he was cut off from the land of the living
Through the sin of my people, who deserved the punishment.
And his grave was set among the wicked.
And with the rich, in his death—
Though he had done no injustice
And had spoken no falsehood.
But the Lord chose to crush him by disease,
That, if he made himself an offering for guilt,
He might see offspring and have long life,

And that through him the Lord's purpose might prosper.
Out of his anguish he shall see it;
He shall enjoy it to the full through his devotion."

I put the scroll back on the shelf. To whom was Isaiah referring?

When Brutus rode away on his horse a little later, I hurried to find Mari. She was laying out clothes on the rocks to dry them.

"Is Shale not coming today? How can Brutus leave on the day of his daughter's arrival?"

Mari sighed. "It's so unfortunate. There has been another uprising and they needed him in Jerusalem."

"So he won't even be here to greet her."

Her eyes met mine in uncharacteristic sadness. "He promised he'd be back as soon as possible. We need to pray for his speedy return."

I nodded.

Mari smiled. "You have a kind heart."

I laughed. Mari was five years older than I was and seemed like a sister. If I had a problem, she was the one I went to see. She had plenty to do without distraction, so I went back to my own mental to-do list.

I couldn't resist keeping a vigil. Every few minutes I'd find an excuse to steal a look down the road. By noon, I had become so preoccupied with her arrival I had not gotten much work done. I imagined a beautiful young woman coming over the hill on a donkey. And then I reminded myself I was setting myself up for disappointment. So I would imagine a fat cow coming over the hill on a donkey—and guessed she'd be somewhere in between.

I soon discovered I wasn't the only one watching. I caught Judd gazing down the road, too, though I pretended I didn't notice, and he seemed to be unaware of me. Or maybe neither of us wanted to acknowledge we were both interested in the same young girl's arrival. The only problem was there was only one girl but there were two of us.

I found myself copying him, washing my hands and combing my hair and looking at my reflection in the water. Since arriving,

I'd grown a beard, which made me look older. Judd was three years younger than me. Maybe my age gave me a competitive advantage.

Still, I imagined a family secret that had something to do with Judd. If my ability to read minds could be that specific, I'd know all the family secrets.

At last, a donkey carrying a young girl appeared in view. When I first spotted them, they were a great distance away, merely a tiny dot on the horizon.

I stood on a rocky outcrop filled with anticipation. As she came nearer, I could see her long brown hair below her head covering. She sat sideways with her legs draped to one side of the donkey—and she wasn't flabby or old.

My heart fluttered. I strained to see what she was wearing—a tasteful flowery, purple dress. Water bottles hung off the sides of the donkey. She must have traveled a long distance to carry that many jugs.

Judd said the donkey's name was Baruch. The animal appeared to be gentle, but I wished he'd speed up a little. He could walk faster if he wanted.

As they neared, I noticed her stomach bulged. Was she pregnant? Oh, no, don't tell me that. My initial excitement at meeting her paled in comparison with my despair that she was pregnant. Maybe that was the secret and no one wanted to say.

After a few minutes of eyestrain fixated on the young girl's belly—and feeling guilty for my preoccupation with that part of her body, I decided she didn't have a bulging stomach. She had shifted, readjusted herself, and something white popped up. Then it moved. I squinted. No, it couldn't be. A rabbit?

Why would a young girl on a long journey be traveling with a rabbit? Forget the rabbit—I wanted to see her face, but her head covering shadowed her features.

I heard someone approaching and turned.

Judd acted nonchalant and cool, like this was any other day. "What are you looking at?" he asked.

"That's our new house guest. Scylla told me to receive her."

Judd squinted as he gazed across the field before turning away. Maybe he wasn't interested in her, but his behavior seemed contradictory.

I couldn't tell if he was glad she was coming or hated the extra work that came with her arrival. I'd have to work on trying to read his mind—after I figured out how to read hers.

As Shale approached, I hid behind the fence. I didn't want to look too anxious. Besides, she would want to meet her father and would be very disappointed that he wasn't here.

The donkey stopped underneath some palm trees next to the road. For whatever reason, he didn't want to go any further. The moment had arrived. I slicked back my brown hair and wiped the perspiration off my face.

As I approached, I couldn't contain my excitement. I should have gone to the bathroom. Her keen eyes latched onto mine and I forced myself not to stare. She was bright and fair, lighter in color than I expected.

Her mannerisms reminded me of her father's, the way she sat on the donkey and followed me with her eyes. She smiled shyly.

Then she looked down, as if checking her dress, smoothing it out with one hand and holding the white rabbit with the other.

I introduced myself in Aramaic, "Can I help you?"

She responded in kind. "I'm pleased to meet you. I'm Shale Snyder."

"Here, let me help you down."

"Thanks," she replied. "It was a long journey and I'm glad to be here."

I lifted the young girl off the animal, taking care not to embarrass her in any way, and set her down. She seemed more concerned about the rabbit than her modesty, clutching the small furry creature.

"I pray you had safe travels."

"Yes, I did." She stretched her body and smoothed her dress below her knees.

"Your father has been expecting you."

A look of surprise fell across her face. "What? What did you say?"

I realized I'd said something I shouldn't. But considering the circumstances, what else should I have said?

I changed the subject. "You've traveled a long distance?"

"Yes. But what did you say about my father?"

At that moment Scylla approached. I was glad she came before I made another faux pas.

Scylla had dolled herself up to impress Shale and walked with an edge of superiority. What a false façade. Could Shale perceive her fakeness?

"How are you, Shale? I'm Scylla, your father's wife. Brutus is expecting you. He'll be back from Jerusalem shortly."

Scylla reached out to shake Shale's hand, much like two political leaders from Israel and Syria would shake hands over a fake peace treaty. I wished Shale's father had been here to greet her.

The young girl was reserved but very observant. Physically she was tall for the girls of this time. Her high cheekbones and long eyelashes made her look like a Hollywood beauty. Maybe she wore mascara—unheard of in first century Palestine—unless you were a person of means.

I knew nothing about her mother. Shale reminded me of the girls back home—a sophisticated worldliness that had its virtues and flaws.

"We missed you, Baruch," said Scylla. She patted the donkey. "I'm glad you're home now."

I was surprised at Scylla's kindness towards the animal although she had always made sure the animals had food and the best care—her one redeeming quality.

"And what about the rabbit?" asked Scylla. "Can my servant take the animal back with Baruch? We have a cave where we keep the animals safe at night, a stable."

Shale hesitated.

I smiled reassuringly. "I can give him some vegetables."

"It's a she," Shale corrected me. "Her name is Cherios."

I squirmed. "Pardon me. Let me take Cherios and Baruch and give them each some food and water."

She relented with my reassurance.

"How about your bag?"

"Bag—yes, but I think I'll hold on to the knapsack."

Shale patted Baruch, the donkey. "See you in a bit, and you, too, Cherios." She handed me a blanket. "If you would take that also."

I led the donkey around to the back, holding the white rabbit underneath my arm.

Judd sat on the rocky ledge that led to the cave's door. Ambivalence shadowed his face. He eyed Baruch with familiarity. "So Shale has arrived?"

I nodded. "Where do I put this donkey?"

Without answering my question, Judd's eyes turned to the rabbit. "She brought a rabbit?"

"Yes."

"I bet he'd taste good in rabbit soup."

I scrawled at him. "Cherios is a pet rabbit, and it's a she."

Judd looked indignant. "So what does Shale look like?" He stood and followed me.

No sooner was the cave door cracked than Much-Afraid bolted. She ran around the yard sniffing the air as if chasing a faint scent. Then she ran back and pawed at Baruch with unveiled excitement. The dog licked Baruch's face and crouched in friendly submission, wagging her tail. Curtsy sashays and whimpers of joy followed. Was this a dog's way of saying, "Welcome home"?

After a few minutes, Much-Afraid ran to the back portico and sat, wagging her tail at the closed door.

How did she know we had a guest? I called her but she ignored me. I put out food—but she didn't even want that. Shale had won over the heart of Much-Afraid without even meeting her—or so I thought.

Judd disappeared just as he was needed—after I realized Much-Afraid wasn't going to leave the back portico. Which stall did he prepare for the donkey? I led the donkey inside the cave, still clutching the rabbit that was now wiggling to be free.

I closed the cave door behind me to make sure she couldn't escape, but I was hesitant to put her down until I could find the right container. We had open wooden crates and water jugs and horse stalls and pigsties, but nothing seemed appropriate for a small white rabbit.

As I sat on the bench holding the animal, the donkey walked towards the middle of the cave and stood in front of a stall.

I opened the gate and Baruch entered. Soon he was munching on fresh feed. Suddenly the rabbit jumped out of my arms and buried herself in the donkey's hay. Baruch leaned over and sniffed. Cherios hopped on his head, scurried up his neck, and plopped down on the donkey's back. The rabbit stared at me bright-eyed wiggling her nose.

Who was I to argue with a donkey and a rabbit? They had already decided where they wanted to be. I didn't need Judd to tell me.

I needed to check on Nathan. Was he still waiting in his room? Since Brutus had left unexpectedly, I wasn't sure if I was to introduce Nathan to Shale.

I closed the cave door and headed back to the house.

Mari saw me through the window and smiled.

When I entered the house, she greeted me. "She's a lovely girl, isn't she?"

I nodded.

She motioned for me to come closer.

"You will be pleased to know that Nathan came down and met the young lady. You had Nathan so well prepared, you would have been proud of him. He acted very mature."

That was a relief. "What's happening now?"

"Shale went up to her room to rest a while. She seemed very tired and wanted a few moments to catch her breath."

I nodded. "So everything seems to be going well?"

"Seems to be," Mari said. "Are you taking care of that rabbit of hers?"

"The rabbit wanted to be with Baruch, so I left them together. I hope that's acceptable."

Mari pointed at the door to step back outside. She closed the door behind us. "Scylla requested that they have a private dinner tonight, just for the family."

I didn't see anything wrong with that. Nathan had met her and I could understand Scylla's desire for privacy, though if Brutus had been here, he would have wanted everyone to eat together.

Mari whispered. "I wanted you to know. I'll keep an eye on Nathan—let you know if I need you."

"Thanks, Mari." I glanced around the back portico, the cave, and the pasture in the distance. "Have you seen Judd?"

"I saw him leaving with his donkey a little bit ago."

"Do you know where they were going?"

Mari shook her head. "I didn't think much of it."

I was probably making much ado about nothing. I turned to leave. Much-Afraid was lying in the portico snoozing. I said as an afterthought, "The dog hasn't left this porch since Shale arrived."

"Do you think she knows Shale from somewhere?" Mari asked.

I frowned. "How could she?"

"Well, I don't know. The dog used to live here at the farm."

I shrugged. "When Shale wakes up, we'll find out more." I laughed. "Maybe Judd ran away."

CHAPTER 18 VENTRILOQUIST

I awoke early the next morning. Sleep eluded me most of the night and now I had a sleep-deprived hangover. I shook it off and climbed the outdoor steps to the flat roof, pausing on the second floor. Was Shale up yet?

I continued to the final rise to enjoy the start of a new day. I chuckled. I needed to be honest—I wanted to satisfy my own curiosity.

I could see the pasture, the cave entrance, and the road bordering the property. Then I saw Shale. What was she doing up so early?

The young girl was traipsing along the well-trodden path to the well. Had Scylla already assigned her chores? What a compassionate stepmother. I hoped Shale would meet her father before Scylla drove her away.

My eyes followed the trail. A figure caught my attention. Who would be at the well this early? That had to be Judd. His donkey was with him. I couldn't mistake the brute for any other.

After disappearing most of yesterday, he had decided to show up at the well to meet Shale—the women's favorite hangout. Did he know she would be coming? Did Scylla clue him in? My thoughts vexed me.

I shrugged. Could I read Judd's mind? Sometimes it happened when I wasn't trying. Urgency to follow Shale made me panic. I ran down the stairs and hurried up the trail. Suddenly Assassin bolted past me. Fear chilled me to the bones. Judd wouldn't hurt Shale, would he?

I reached the top of the hill and saw Shale's back. A scowl covered Judd's face and an empty bucket lay on the ground. Water saturated the wet soil and dripped from Judd's cloak.

Shale pointed her finger, saying in an accusing voice, "You're a liar."

Judd smirked. "You've come back."

He glared at me. I crept up behind Shale.

Shale's voice quivered. "What are you talking about?"

She backed into me as Judd approached. She turned, surprised but relieved. "Daniel."

"What's going on?" I asked.

Judd mumbled a few unintelligible words and took off after his donkey.

Shale's eyes questioned me. "Where did you come from?"

"I don't know you well enough to explain."

Shale twitched. "What's that supposed to mean?"

I watched Judd disappear in the distance. I glanced at the overturned bucket and avoided Shale's question. "What did he do to you?"

She turned away. "I don't want to talk about it, but thanks for coming."

I filled the bucket and we headed back to the house in silence. When we arrived, I waited to see if she wanted to talk, but she didn't.

I'd learn to read her mind. Some people were more extroverted than others. I sensed Shale was an introvert.

I set the heavy bucket down. "After you eat breakfast, come find me in the cave if you want to talk about it."

Shale nodded. I left her standing in the portico hoping she would come. In my new reality, I had met a girl to whom I was very attracted.

I strolled out to the pasture. When I tried to open the gate, however, I couldn't lift the handle. It was jammed. I jiggled it several times and finally the latch gave way. The door squeaked as I pushed it open, as if it hadn't been open in years. I didn't remember an issue with the gate.

When I looked ahead, the field was bathed in morning sunlight. A dozen or more sheep grazed on the hill.

Behind them, at the top of the crest, I saw a dark figure. I walked in that direction to get a better look. When I approached, I saw the old woman. She was dressed in the same attire, walking on the ridge in bare feet, chanting unintelligible words and throwing flowers over the hill.

She stopped her strange activity when she saw me. She pulled out a flower from the bouquet and thrust it at me. "The corpse flower," she said.

I took the miniature flower without thinking and breathed in the scent. The flower smelled like rotting flesh. My eyes burned. I threw the flower on the ground.

"You are still looking," she said.

"The flower smells like a decomposing body."

She didn't say anything but continued walking. I trailed behind her. I wanted to remove my contacts and rub my eyes, but I'd have to wait. I couldn't risk losing them in the field. I blinked several times but the burning continued.

She tried to hand me another flower, but I shook my head.

The woman smiled. Some people shouldn't smile.

"You found me again," she said

"Why are you following me?" I asked.

"This is where I live," the old woman said, "in the spiritual realm." She flicked another flower on the ground. "Do you know where you are?"

I did not trust this old woman. "No, I don't," I replied. "Tell me."

"You are in a different reality."

Like that meant something to me. "What different reality?"

"It's a spiritual reality," she said. "I'm a ventriloquist."

What did that make me?

She continued. "My boss rules over all the kingdoms of the earth." The old woman threw another flower on the ground and continued to chant in a singsong voice.

"Why don't you speak in a language I know?"

"I am. You can hear me."

This woman was crazy. Who was her boss? "I believe in the God of Abraham. He rules over all the earth."

When she heard me, fire filled the old woman's eyes.

She scoffed. "So you believe in God, do you?"

"Yes."

"You don't act like it," she chided me. She did a twirling dance holding the flowers. Then she stopped and faced me.

"What has your belief in God gotten you? A missing father, a dead mentor, a dead sister—"

I interrupted her. "What do you mean, a dead sister? And how do you know about my father and mentor? Is Martha injured?"

The old woman said, "Watch." She threw another flower over the ledge. The plant magically rooted and shot up from the ground. The leaves opened and a helix appeared. Mother and Martha were asleep. Only a few minutes had passed while I had spent five months in first century Palestine.

"Your mother and sister are sleeping," she said.

I was relieved, but her comment bothered me. I didn't know what she meant.

"You want to get back home?"

Now I wasn't sure. A young woman had entered my world. I hesitated. "Who are you?"

"I have magic." She threw the last flower over the hill. "But I can't violate your free will."

"Why do you talk so cryptically?"

"I'm very patient," the old woman said, "for those I want." She laughed. Her decaying teeth seemed worse than before.

"If you have so much power, you should do something about your appearance."

"If I were beautiful, you would want something different." She quit smiling. "I know you better than you know yourself."

She turned her back to me, chanting again as she walked away.

I followed her. "Tell me who you are,"

She stopped and faced me. "I told you, I'm a ventriloquist. Life is about choices, and I'm giving you a very desirable choice."

I grew impatient. "Tell me who you really are."

"Your benefactor." She kept walking.

I gave up. My eyes were killing me. Maybe she was the witch of Endor. I didn't want her as my benefactor. I vowed to stay away from her and not talk to her again.

CHAPTER 19 CONVERSATIONS

I hurried back to the cave. I'd spent too much time talking to the strange woman and needed to wash my eyes.

When I opened the door, Shale was waiting for me with Cherios in her arms. Much-Afraid stood wagging her tail beside the last stall. I picked up a cloth and wiped off my hands. I wanted to wash my eyes, but I was worried about the contacts. I didn't want to do it in front of Shale.

Her stoic mannerisms from earlier gave way to a warmth I didn't know she had. She walked over to the bench, sat at the table, and smiled.

I joined her on the other side. "So how was breakfast?"

"Fine," Shale said. The smile left her face as fleetingly as it had appeared. "I'm not happy Judd put Baruch in the small stall in the back. That's not Baruch's old stall. Can't you put him up here where he belongs?"

For all the things she could be upset about, I couldn't believe she was making a fuss over the donkey's stall.

"Does it matter? They are all about the same." I could think of reasons to argue with Judd but worrying about the stall seemed irrelevant.

Shale wanted no part of my ambivalence. "Aren't you in charge here?"

"Well, I suppose, but Judd knows how to provide for the animals. He's been doing it a lot longer than I have. That was the stall the animal chose anyway."

Shale was rigid. "Why are you siding with him? Why can't we move him to this stall?" She pointed to the one near us.

"It's not as if he's being abused."

Shale scrunched her nose. "I don't like that Baruch is in the back, but if that's the way you feel, fine." She crossed her arms defiantly.

What a fiery young woman. She must have gotten that from her mother. Shale's father never got upset about anything.

I tried to calm her. "We can move him."

My eyes burned so much I had to rub them. I really needed to take out the contacts.

Shale studied my face. "Is something in your eye?"

"No, it's not that." Why had I taken that flower from the ventriloquist?

I leaned over and one of my contacts fell on the table. I scooped it up hoping Shale hadn't seen it. Not that she would know what it was, but she was too observant.

"What was that?" Shale asked.

"Nothing."

"Is that a contact lens?"

"What?"

"The thing in your hand," she said impatiently.

"No," I lied.

A look of disbelief crossed her face. She leaned forward. Her face looked blurry and I didn't like being interrogated.

"Where do you come from?" she demanded.

Too many questions crossed my mind. Could Shale be from the future? Maybe she didn't belong here either. I was afraid to say anything that might scare her. I didn't need a fourteen-year-old girl fainting. What would I think in 2015 if a man told me he was from my future? If she were from first century Palestine, she would probably be terrified of me.

"How perceptive you are," I replied.

Shale rolled her eyes.

"How do you know what this is?"

The young girl stood and spread out her palms. "Come on, you're the one with the contact lens, not me."

I tried again. "Tell me about your family."

96

Shale exploded. "Are you kidding?" She plopped down in the chair, shaking her head. "Men," I heard her say under her breath.

I leaned on the table and rubbed my eyes, but that only made them burn more. Then I stood and paced. If she got this upset about little things, what would she think if I told her the truth?

I tried to make sense of it. How would she know about contact lenses if she were from around here? She might know if she were from somewhere else. I stared at her. When were contact lenses invented?

"I need to be able to trust you," I said.

She lowered her voice. "You can trust me."

Shale's eyes focused on Judd's donkey. "Wait a minute. Can you put Assassin to pasture?"

"Assassin?" I wasn't sure anyone knew his name except me. It's not as if you share a name like that.

"How do you know his name?"

"He told me," replied Shale.

"Judd told you?"

"No, the donkey told me."

"The donkey told you?"

Shale grimaced. "Well, sort of."

I had gone from speaking to someone who seemed like a witch to someone who claimed to be able to talk to animals. Maybe I was the crazy one.

"I'll put him outside. Wait here."

I returned a few minutes later, leaving the door ajar. After my unfortunate encounter with Scylla, I didn't want to be alone with Shale. She seemed a little strange.

"Don't you want to close the door? Someone might hear us."

I shrugged. "No one else is around." In reality, I knew Judd was nearby, but I didn't want him making up stories about us. Next thing you know, he'd be accusing me of worse things.

Shale was unhappy with the door open, but stopped complaining. I sat at the table and focused on the young girl's face. I especially like her deep-set round eyes. Even if she were a little weird, I liked her.

"So you can talk to animals?"

She hesitated. "Yes, I can talk to animals and they can talk to me."

I scratched the back of my neck and leaned forward in my chair. Did I believe her? Whether she could or not, she believed she could.

"Have you always been able to talk to animals?"

Shale shook her head. "Someone called my name. That was the first time."

Much-Afraid padded over and sat beside Shale. She scratched the dog's ear. "The first voice I heard was hers—before I was transported to the garden."

I glanced at Much-Afraid. "What garden?"

"The king's garden."

I sighed. Was Shale dreaming up stories? What about me? I'd had some strange encounters, too. I couldn't talk to animals, I hadn't been to a garden, but I could read minds—a little, and I had a ventriloquist following me around who gave me the willies, and somehow I had been transported back in time two thousand years.

Maybe we were both crazy. I rubbed my chin. "Why don't you tell me where you come from?"

She laughed. "You really want to know?"

I nodded.

"Are you sure?"

"Yes, I'm sure."

She sighed. "Okay. Here goes."

CHAPTER 20 WORLD OF SHALE

S hale hugged the rabbit in her lap, closed her eyes, and seemed to concentrate. I lingered on her face and studied her features.

"I don't live here," she began. She reopened her eyes. "Have you ever heard of the United States?"

I chuckled. "Are you an American?"

Shale nodded.

A teen from the United States. How was it possible that we could find each other in the past, when we both came from the future? I stared at her without realizing it.

She waved her hand in front of me. "Are you okay?"

I shook my head. "This is just too weird. How could we be here?"

"I know," Shale agreed. "But it's sure nice to meet someone here from 2013."

"I'm from 2015."

"Really?"

I had so many questions, I didn't know which to ask first. She couldn't know Aramaic or Hebrew. "Can you understand me?"

Shale giggled. "I'm talking to you, aren't I?"

I followed the edges of the cave to the back. "Shale," I said slowly, "I'm speaking to you in Aramaic and I'm hearing you in Aramaic."

"No, you aren't. You're speaking to me in English and I'm speaking to you in English. Everyone around here speaks in English," she insisted.

I shook my head. I switched to English. "Do I sound any different?"

"No. Should you?"

How could that be? We were hearing each other in our own language. I could probably speak to her in Hebrew and she'd understand me just as well. I remembered what the old woman had said. Maybe we were in a different reality.

"Keep going," I urged her. "I want to hear your story."

Shale leaned over and kissed the rabbit. Cherios cooed.

"What did the rabbit say?" I meant it as a joke but Shale didn't.

"She said to make sure I tell you about the king."

"The king?"

"The king of the garden. Now shush. Be quiet."

I chuckled. "I promise to be quiet."

Shale patted Much-Afraid as the dog leaned in close to her—as if she didn't want to miss a word of Shale's story.

"I suppose it all started with Much-Afraid." Shale glanced down at the dog. "I was having problems in school—kids bullying me. My mom had remarried. No one understood me, including my mom or my stepfather."

Shale gulped in a deep breath of stale cave air. "Even the teachers at school needled me."

She looked away. "I did have one friend, Rachel, but when a pervert attacked me in the hallway and I set him straight, I was expelled. Rachel wasn't allowed to be my friend anymore."

My mind went to 2015. The evening news was filled with such stories. That didn't happen here—at least I'd never heard about it.

Shale shifted in her chair. I remained still so I wouldn't interrupt her thoughts.

Shale shared her story in minute detail. Then she brought up her father and told me about a gift she had received from him. Her eyes lit up when she explained about the appearance of a strange dog that wanted to be her friend—but the apartment where she lived wouldn't allow her to keep the animal.

"Where was God in all of this?" she asked.

I understood her feelings. Where was God when you needed him?

Shale stroked Cherios. "I followed the dog into the woods and something happened. I don't remember what, except that I fell and was knocked out. When I came to, I saw Much-Afraid. She reminded me of the animal from my favorite children's story, *The Donkey and the King*.

Shale squinted. "It was as if something from my past that was meaningful came alive. Maybe I clung to that because I wanted to believe that something or somebody cared about me."

Shale shrugged. "The dog didn't leave me, but she was far away. I couldn't touch her."

Much-Afraid nudged Shale's hand and whimpered.

"Yes, I'm getting to that. Just wait."

Shale laughed. "Winter came alive like Christmas. You know how it is when you're in a beautiful dream and the alarm goes off? For a brief instant, before the dream leaves you, you hate to wake up."

I nodded.

"It was like that. Three white doves landed on me. They cooed, though I couldn't understand them. I guess I couldn't talk to animals yet. I knew they wanted to help me. They kissed the wound on my head. A pulsating light made beautiful music. The sounds radiated from the ground and then all around."

Shale waved her hand. "As mysteriously as the doves came, they flew away. When I looked up, multi-colored lights led to an open door. Diamonds sparkled around the opening. I wanted to enter the door, but I wasn't sure if I could put weight on my ankle."

I glanced down at Shale's leg and ankle and admired her slender lines.

Shale smiled at Much-Afraid. "I heard the voice for the first time. "Are you okay?" she asked me. I couldn't tell where the voice came from. I looked for the dog, but I didn't see her."

Shale laughed. "That's when I named her Much-Afraid—the character from the children's story. I sensed she was nearby."

Shale stopped. "Are you sure you want to hear all of this?"

"Yes, I do. Please keep going."

Shale continued. "As the light faded, the door became more visible, and I saw Much-Afraid.

"I wasn't sure if the voice was hers—I mean, I had never heard a dog talk, but no one was around. The light was beautiful, but different. The bubbles of many colors bounced—I had no fear at all."

Shale's experience was more uplifting than mine was.

She laughed. "I told Much-Afraid to wait. I caught up to her, but she slipped through my fingers.

"You still want me to keep going?"

"Please."

Shale took another breath.

Much-Afraid stood on her hind legs and nudged Shale's arm.

"Yes, now I know it was you, but I didn't know then."

The dog whimpered and plopped on the floor with her ears straight up. The magic of the moment confounded me.

Shale continued. "I followed Much-Afraid through the door and arrived at a beautiful garden. Bright-colored flowers covered the rolling hills and cascading vines clung to hanging walls—and the air was pure, as if you could taste it."

Shale closed her eyes. "The garden seemed perfect, but I discovered it wasn't all beautiful. Something evil wanted me. Does that sound weird?"

"No."

Shale bit her lip. "I had a secret that kept coming to mind, something I wanted to forget. So in this beautiful garden, something evil kept bringing up this thing I didn't want to remember."

Shale shrugged. "I was afraid, but I didn't know how to get back. I heard voices."

The young girl glanced at Cherios. "I followed the voices and that's when I stumbled on Cherios and Baruch."

Shale giggled. "Imagine this. The two of them were lounging under an apple tree, without a care in the world. They were talking as we are. I couldn't believe I understood what they were saying."

I smiled.

Shale stroked Cherios' head. "Yes, you gave me a beautiful flower."

"Anyway, I'm making this story way too long, but it is a beautiful story." A look of resignation crossed her face. "In the garden, things were not as they appeared. Dark creatures had invaded. Both Baruch and Cherios were terrified of them."

Shale became sad. "I couldn't understand how such a beautiful garden could be tainted. The vile creatures smelled like rotten eggs, decaying carcasses. I was frightened witless when they chased us from the garden."

I remembered the stink of the bag woman—it was the smell of rotten eggs.

Shale shuddered. "We barely escaped. If it hadn't been for Baruch, I guess I would have been eaten."

I thought about Shale's story. Were our experiences related in some way? "What happened then?"

Shale shared the rest of her story. As she spoke, I began to understand how Much-Afraid knew Shale.

Shale snickered. "When I discovered I was back in time, I nearly fainted. I had bought a dress and when the woman handed me the change, I saw the image of Julius Caesar on the coin. How can anyone go back in time thousands of years, for goodness' sake?"

I shook my head. "I don't know."

Shale's face turned serious and her eyes widened. "But that wasn't the biggest surprise."

"What was the biggest surprise?"

Shale giggled. "When you helped me off the donkey and told me my father was expecting me."

I gulped.

Shale sighed. "The father I never knew—and still don't know. Even in this world, my father doesn't care about me."

"That's not true, Shale. Don't think that." What else could I say?

"But I have a stinking stepmother." Shale laughed. "Just my luck."

Shale picked at the fur on Cherios' head. "Sorry, that wasn't very nice."

I let the comment go. "So where does Judd fit into this?"

The color left Shale's face. She flinched and shook her head. "Later."

I'd have to wait to find out that part.

Shale continued. "After meeting my stepmother, I went up to my room and fell asleep. I don't know how long I slept, maybe an hour, and in my dream I heard a dog barking."

Shale glanced at Much-Afraid. "Guess who I heard?"

I nodded. I leaned back comparing Shale's story with mine. How did they fit together? I hadn't been to a garden. Our stories weren't the same, but we had both arrived at the same place in the first century.

Shale touched my arm. "You don't think I'm crazy, do you?"

Her words jarred me. "Shale, you're not crazy. If you were, I would know. I was in a psychiatric ward."

She pulled away. "What?" she blurted out, "Tell me you aren't psycho."

I had overstated my case. "Relax."

Shale composed herself, much to my relief. How much did I want to tell her? She had been open but didn't reveal all of her secrets.

"Where should I start?"

Shale said, "Why don't you begin by telling me how you have contact lenses when we are in a place without iPhones or TVs or toilets that flush. What are you holding back on me?"

She was right. "First I need to put this in my eye." I walked towards the back to get some water. It would give me a moment to compose my thoughts. If I said too much, would she reject me—or be bored?

I returned to the table and began. "Your father will be here soon. Things are not as they appear. I mean, you're confused, right?"

Shale nodded. "That's an understatement."

I told her about my past, that I was two or three years into her future, and my thoughts about more than one reality or place existing at the same time.

I shared a little about my family. I couldn't bring myself to talk about my father's disappearance, since Shale had her own father to worry about.

When I told her about Dr. Luke, she interrupted me. "You know Doctor Luke?"

"Yes. You say that as if you know him."

"I saw him yesterday in a small town on the way here."

"Strange you would see him also."

Shale nodded.

I went on to explain how I arrived at her father's house and came to be a mentor to Nathan. "So here I am," I finished, "wondering why I'm here and how I will ever get back."

Shale laughed. "That makes two of us. Maybe we were supposed to meet."

I noticed Judd in the doorway. What had he done to cause her such anxiety? When she realized Judd had been eavesdropping, I explained, "He's not the same Judd from your own time. He's a counterpart—he didn't go through a door and travel to this world as we've done."

"What do you mean?" she asked.

"I don't get it either," I admitted.

Shale shook her head as if disagreeing with me. "He has to be the same person."

"He's the same person, but it's as if we're in a parallel universe. Suppose you had been born in this time and in this country? This would be your world."

"I still don't understand," Shale confessed.

"I'm not sure I do either, but some things seem to stay the same."

Shale's eyes narrowed. "Like what?"

I remembered the ventriloquist's words. Could there be a connection? "Maybe we are here to make choices, deal with personal problems."

"That's philosophical," Shale said. "So my father is my problem?"

"Perhaps."

"What's yours?"

That was a loaded question. Would I tell her even if I knew? "My family isn't here except for a sister who owns a small shop in Dothan. At least I haven't met anyone else. I'm related in some way to Mari, but she won't tell me how."

Shale glanced at Cherios and shot a look at Baruch, who was still in the back stall. "The animals—they keep talking about a king."

"I don't know anything about a king, except—"

"Except what?"

I hesitated. "I don't know if it's a coincidence, but many years ago Herod killed all the babies in Bethlehem—believing a king had been born in the small town."

Shale readjusted herself on the bench, still clutching Cherios. "What do you mean, he killed all the babies? Why?"

"He was afraid another king would take over—the prophets predicted a king would come from Bethlehem and that was King Herod's territory."

I added, "When you put it into historical context, it's a little eerie. I mean, I know in first century Israel a false prophet came on the scene that many called a king—Yeshua of Nazareth."

Shale glanced away, as if becoming bored by my historical references, and changed the subject abruptly. She clasped her hands and said excitedly with a twinkle in her eye. "So tell me about you. You said you come from 2015—I want to hear all about 2015 and where you live."

My father was still alive in 2012. So much had changed. I grimaced. "I wouldn't want to be you and relive the last three years."

Shale's eyes widened. "What do you mean?"

I told her about the deepening rift between Israel and the United States, the threat of war, and rising tensions. I followed it up with the words, "When you reject God, bad things happen. Judgment always follows."

I studied the ground, as I felt conflicted. Did I believe that? I wasn't sure what I believed anymore.

Shale's voice brought me back to the present. "You scare me, Daniel. I don't know if I ever want to go back."

I sighed. "It's not like we're in paradise here." My words hung over us. Could we both get back to our own time and be friends— or maybe more?

I glanced at the door and lowered my voice so Judd couldn't hear. "Where in the U.S. are you from?"

"Atlanta, Georgia."

I smiled. I remembered the picture of my cousin on our refrigerator. "I have a distant relative who lives there. I doubt that you would know her, though."

"Who is it?" Shale asked.

"Rachel Franco."

Shale's face lit up. "You're kidding me. Rachel is my best friend."

I stared at Shale. "Wow! That's unbelievable. Is that the same Rachel who couldn't be your friend?"

Shale nodded. "Yes."

There were so many coincidences.

Shale reached her hand across the table and touched my arm. "Daniel, do you miss home?"

I nodded. "I especially miss my computer."

Shale nodded. "Me, too. Toilets and showers"—she smirked and rolled her eyes—"any running water. I hate that I have to fetch water every day. Women spend far too much time doing stupid, mundane things here."

I laughed.

Her eyes grew big. "I'll never complain about emptying the dishwasher again."

I nodded. "I'd sure like to take in a soccer game."

Shale giggled. "I'm not much into soccer, but a baseball game would be great, with a couple of hotdogs layered with mustard and ketchup, and then fireworks after the game."

"We actually have a national baseball team in Israel now, though I've never been to a game."

Shale yawned. "A strong cup of coffee from Starbucks would be awesome. I hate getting up so early."

We both laughed.

"That old witch made me get up at the crack of dawn to fetch a pail of water."

I nodded. "I know."

The smile left her lips. I bet she was remembering Judd. Could I think of a way to get her mind off him? Her spunkiness was uplifting. I wanted to spend more time with her, but approaching hoof beats interrupted our conversation.

"Your father is here."

"Really? How do you know?"

"I perceive things. Like this morning at the well. How do you think I knew something was wrong?"

Shale shook her head. "I don't know."

I stood. "Come and meet your father—maybe one of the reasons why you're here. By the way, your father is a kind man."

"Thanks," Shale said.

I took Cherios from her and put the rabbit in the stall with Baruch. Shale followed me outside. The brightness was blinding after being in the dark cave. Brutus had tethered his horse to the post. Shale touched my arm.

I put my hand on her shoulder. "If you wait, I'll introduce you—if it would make you less nervous. Right now I need to feed and water Brutus's horse."

Shale nodded, as if she were willing to wait for me.

Suddenly a crow appeared on the far post of the portico. He flapped his wings and screeched annoyingly. I glanced at Shale who seemed focused on the bird.

"You think I should go inside—he's waiting for me?" she asked.

The crow screeched back.

"Are you talking to that crow?" I asked.

Shale nodded.

I shook my head in disbelief.

Suddenly the bird flew away.

Shale smiled, but didn't say anything.

I glanced around. Where was Judd when you needed him? I walked Brutus's horse to the trough for fresh water and food. When I returned to the portico, Shale had already gone inside. I stood outside the door and remembered my father.

CHAPTER 21 CONFRONTATION

I cracked the door open but couldn't hear anything. I was reluctant to eavesdrop on what should be a private reunion between the two of them. I decided to go back to the cave. Now that I knew what the animals meant to Shale, I wanted to put Baruch in the front stall and move Assassin to the back. No sooner had I done so than Judd opened the door to the cave. When he saw the switch, he fumed. "What'd you do that for?"

"That's Baruch's old stall."

"How do you know?"

I picked up a bucket and hung it on the wall. "I just know."

Judd frowned. "How did you hit it off with Brutus's daughter?"

"What?" I asked.

Judd ignored my question. "Whatever she told you isn't true."

"She didn't tell me anything about you."

Judd shrugged.

"Why were you at the well?" I asked.

"I don't have to tell you," Judd said tersely.

He walked to the back and poured Assassin some oats. I tried to read his mind.

Judd sneered, "So did you lie with her, like you did Brutus's wife?"

I shook my head. "I never did any such thing with Scylla. Shale and I are just friends."

Judd's jealousy ballooned. "I don't believe you. You've had your eyes on her since the day she arrived."

I stared at him. "Is that the only way you can look at a young woman?"

Judd glowered. "Family secrets. You'll find out soon enough."

"Like what?"

Judd got in my face. "Stay away from her."

I shoved him back. I didn't need a fourteen-year-old kid treating me like a turd.

Judd stormed out of the cave, slamming the door. I waited a few minutes before leaving, to make sure he was gone.

A short while later, Shale and her father walked outside the house to sit in the portico. I wandered over to say "hi." Brutus was smiling and Shale seemed upbeat. We made small talk before they proceeded down the road. Memories of my father returned, pleasant times on holiday when I was young.

As I watched Shale and her father in the distance, I lamented my father's disappearance. Suddenly I longed to visit Dr. Luke, but I also worried about Shale and her animals. And why was she so afraid of Judd?

CHAPTER 22 MISSING

T he next day I stared into Baruch's empty stall. I ran over and checked to see if Judd had switched the donkeys, but Assassin was still where I'd put him. At least Shale's dog and rabbit were in the cave. The animals followed me around. The dog's favorite pig was squealing. What was his problem?

I would have to find out what Judd knew. I mumbled to myself a few choice words as I tromped to his quarters.

I banged on the door. "Are you there? I need to talk to you."

When he didn't respond, I rattled the handle. I'd about given up when the door opened.

Judd looked through the crack, sleepy-eyed. "What is it?"

"Open up, will you?"

He cracked it more.

I grabbed his collar and pulled him close to me. "Did you do something to that donkey?"

"What donkey?"

I let go of him. "You know what donkey—Baruch."

Judd straightened his tunic, squinting in the sun. "I just woke up. I don't know what you're talking about."

I forced the door open and looked around his room.

"Baruch is missing."

"He's probably out in the pasture."

I shook my head. "No."

Judd stepped out and ran towards the cave. We inspected each stall and then checked the pasture. The donkey wasn't anywhere.

Judd said, "Someone could have stolen him, though I don't know why. It's not like he's a prize animal." He scratched his eyebrow. "Is Shale here?"

I remembered I hadn't seen her since yesterday. "I don't know. I assume she is."

"Maybe we better check," Judd said.

I didn't think she would go off with Baruch and leave Much-Afraid and Cherios behind.

When we entered the back portico, Mari asked, "Is Shale with you?"

Judd said, "No."

I shook my head. "Baruch is missing."

Mari appeared worried.

I still didn't believe she would take off without good reason. "We need to tell Brutus."

Who was going to volunteer?

I heard horses approaching. "Is Brutus expecting visitors?"

"I don't think so," Mari said.

We walked to the side gate. Two Roman soldiers galloped towards us.

"I'll get Brutus," Mari said. She turned and went inside.

The soldiers tied up their horses. "We need to see Brutus," one of the Roman guards said.

I motioned for them to follow and took them to his study. "Wait here and he'll be with you soon."

When Brutus entered, he and the soldier spoke in Latin, which made it difficult to follow the conversation.

Mari whispered, "Let's go outside."

Judd was still looking for clues.

"So as not to alarm Brutus, I told him that Baruch and Shale had gone for a morning walk. It could be nothing," she reassured me.

That was true. Maybe I had panicked.

Scylla walked out and joined us. "Is something going on? Why is the cave door open?"

"Judd, I thought you closed the door," I said.

"Don't go blaming everything on me now."

In the pasture, Much-Afraid was chasing sheep. Cherios sat preening on the bench.

"Put the animals in the cave and tell Shale to come see me, please," Scylla said to no one in particular.

"Shale isn't here," Judd said. "And Baruch is missing."

Scylla's face turned ashen. "Find them."

She stormed back inside yelling at me, "Daniel, if you can't do your job, we'll find someone who can."

No one said anything, but it seemed odd she was more concerned about the donkey than about Shale. A few minutes later, Brutus took off with the Roman soldiers, promising to be back as soon as he could.

"Extend my apologies to Shale for leaving on such short notice." He added, "I'm sure she's fine. Just like me, can't stay in one spot for too long without getting antsy."

I worried the rest of the day. Was it because I knew her better than anyone else? She didn't know the dangers that existed here, and she certainly didn't know the area. I drove myself insane thinking about all the bad things that could happen.

Scylla called me into her room late in the afternoon when Shale hadn't returned.

"Did you say something to her that drove her away?" she asked. "Did you do something to her?"

I shook my head. She looked out her bedroom window. "Search the road and the hills around the property. Maybe she fell, had an accident."

I did as she suggested, but didn't find her anywhere.

The sun was setting when Shale returned with Baruch. I ran out to the road to greet her.

"Where have you been?"

"Long story," she replied. "I'll tell you later."

I took Baruch and led him to the stable. Judd washed down the donkey and cooled him off. I noted the poor animal was dirty, tired, and thirsty.

"They must have been down in the wilderness," Judd said. "Baruch is very dehydrated. Why would they have gone down there?"

I shrugged. "I'm just glad they're safe."

Now that Shale and Baruch were back, the distance between Judd and me widened again. I was worried. Had I said something to Shale that upset her? What did Judd tell Scylla? One thing I did know, Shale would feel abandoned by her father if he didn't soon return.

And another thing concerned me. Whatever mind reading ability I once possessed had left me, but I didn't know why. One day I had it and the next day I didn't.

CHAPTER 23 COMPROMISE

Hundreds of birds flew over the Sea of Galilee. They rode invisible currents as easily as I walked along the seashore. I picked up a pebble and threw it into the water. The ripples spanned out and lapped against the rocks. I had brought Nathan with me. He loved to run into the water holding up his tunic, peering into the receding waves looking for fish underneath the surface. Perhaps he found a connection with them. They couldn't speak either.

I was thankful to have some quiet time away from Brutus's home. I had lost the ability to communicate with Nathan in an extraordinary way. Feeling discouraged, I sought solace.

I didn't know whether to tell anyone. Plus I was too upset about my last conversation with Shale to think about much of anything.

"Nathan, I'm going to walk up to that embankment and then I'll come back, all right?"

Nathan nodded and waved.

"Don't go anywhere. I'll be watching you."

He nodded again.

I walked along the shoreline. I noted the sun was behind me and a second shadow came up alongside my own, but no one was near me. When I stopped, the second shadow stopped.

"Can you see me now?"

I turned. I saw the old woman. She was wearing the same dress. Her balding head, hollow eyes, and sunken cheekbones

117

seemed even grimmer in the bright sunshine. She had three fish speared on the end of a stick in her right hand.

"How come I couldn't see you at first?" I asked her.

"I was here," she said.

I shrugged.

"Where are you going?" she asked.

"I'm headed over to the embankment. I need to keep an eye on Nathan."

The old woman came closer and the familiar smell of rotten eggs turned my stomach.

I trekked to the stone embankment that butted into the water as she followed me. Then I climbed to the top to get a better view, keeping my eyes on Nathan. The old woman stayed down below.

I sat on the ledge. "Who are you?"

"I'm your benefactor," she said.

"Come on," I objected. "You aren't my benefactor." I rubbed my nose—what was that foul smell? Must be the dead fish. I tapped myself on the head. "Are you okay—up here?"

The old woman laughed. "What do you want?"

I shifted my weight on the ledge. "I want my gift back," as if I expected her to understand what I meant.

"To read minds?"

I swallowed hard. How did she know?

"I can give you that ability," she said.

I looked at the strange old woman skeptically. "I don't believe you."

She laughed "You are upset with Shale. She's met a man she calls the king, the one Christians call Jesus the Christ. You are troubled because you're in first century Palestine. You are disturbed about events surrounding Yeshua and want to convince Shale he's a charlatan. Is that enough?"

A sick feeling came over me. "How do you know these things?"

"Does it matter?" Her eyes twitched menacingly.

I stared at the fish on the end of her fishing pole.

"So you can give me back the ability to read Nathan's mind?"

"Anyone's mind," she corrected me.

I looked across the water. Why did this bother me when so much good could come out of it? Nathan's life would be more fulfilling and I would know things that Scylla and Judd had kept from me. And I could be a better friend to Shale. Still, I hesitated.

The woman keyed in on my thoughts. "Daniel, you are trying to be a better friend. Let me help you. I told you I was your benefactor."

"What's the cost?"

The woman laughed.

Something about the woman bothered me. She seemed evil. Finally I said, "I need to head back," but I couldn't resist thinking about the offer.

I scooted down the rock wall with her trailing me. Before I reached Nathan, she said, "Nathan is hungry, but you wouldn't know that without being able to read his mind, would you?"

I stopped. All right. "What do I need to do to get the power back?"

"It's done," the old woman said.

When I turned, she was gone, as if she had never been with me. I saw only one shadow.

Was it true? I came up to Nathan. "Hey, are you hungry?"

He nodded and a smile crossed his face. I reached over and squeezed his shoulder. "Come on, let's head back."

CHAPTER 24 DIFFERENCES

E leven Months Later

The days blurred into months. My mind-reading ability had become second nature and I hadn't seen the strange woman again. Each day I tried to finish my chores early so I could spend time in the pasture with Shale—if she had time to join me.

She would generally search for me in the late afternoons—this had become our daily routine. Sunlight filtered through the trees and shone on us in scattered shadows.

Shale held Cherios in her lap and patted the rabbit's back. Much-Afraid had become an expert sheepherder. Judd had invested lots of time teaching the dog. Because Much-Afraid did Judd's work, his slothfulness was less obvious.

Baruch grazed nearby and Lowly the pig had been let out to pasture—at Shale's request, though I insisted he stay far away. Shale didn't care that he was an unclean animal. To her, he was a cute pig with a curly tail, as she described him.

Sometimes I'd ask her what Cherios or one of the animals had said, but I'd gotten used to being left out. Shale hinted that it annoyed her, like asking someone what happened in a movie that is ending. No one wants to tell you.

Judd always watched us—and I usually knew what he was thinking, but I didn't care. I'd never kissed Shale or been alone with her—she was three years younger. Relations were forbidden before betrothal.

I worried more about something else I had discovered. There was a secret contract, a betrothal document between Judd and Shale. I'd overheard Judd and Scylla talking about it one afternoon. Could it be broken? I'd thought about searching for it in Scylla's quarters so I could read it, but I was hopeful the contract would just go away or Judd would change his mind. Probably wishful thinking on my part, but it was like the big elephant in the room no one wanted to talk about—it was there, but no one mentioned it. Certainly Shale had never mentioned it to me.

Whether the contract was real or not, I knew if I defiled her, she would be shamed—could even be stoned. In the meantime, I had grown to love Shale—surpassed only by Judd's envy. He did nothing to conceal his jealousy. He didn't have to. His name was on the contract.

Recently, however, the sweet conversations between Shale and me had become contentious. I sensed restlessness in her. Her father had only been back once. I knew she wanted a relationship with him, but that was hard to do when she was in Galilee and he was somewhere else.

Shale's longings were also spiritual. When her thoughts went there, I'd pushed her away. My interest in spiritual things had evaporated. Shale's had only deepened. The gap between us had widened—not to Judd but to something more disquieting

As we sat in the pasture, Shale was absorbed in her latest drawing. I glanced over to see her artwork.

Two beings faced each other on top of a mountain. One was large and wore a black robe that unfurled across half the mountain. The other was just an ordinary, frail-looking man, half the size of the black creature. I leaned back and stretched. "Are you still thinking about that experience?"

Shale quipped. "I heard some women talking the other day in the village when I went shopping with Mari." She studied her drawing. "I think they were talking about this man."

"What makes you say that?" I asked.

Shale added shading to the dark creature. "They were discussing an itinerant rabbi who stays in Galilee when he isn't teaching. One woman said he was a brilliant rabbi. Another woman called him a prophet. Still another person said she saw him heal her uncle, a paraplegic."

"Who do you say he is?" I asked.

Shale focused her eyes on my face and spoke without hesitation. "I think he is the son of God."

I rolled my eyes. "That's a pretty bold assumption."

The distance between us widened.

Shale was undeterred. "I was in the garden. I know this isn't all there is. I saw him fight the darkness in the wilderness." She bit her lip. "I wish I could see him again. Would you take me if I found out where he is?"

I should have known not to get involved with a girl who wasn't Jewish. I probed around in the dry dirt with a stick. "I don't know what I believe anymore."

Shale shrugged. "Some things are worse than dying."

"Like what?"

"Being alone."

"You aren't alone. I'm here."

"No, Daniel. I'm not alone. But you are."

I sat up straighter. "What do you mean?"

"When I first met you, I was intrigued by your Jewishness—your spirituality. I grew up in a home where we didn't believe in anything. I envied Rachel's family, and when I met you, I saw that passion.

"You've walked away from your past. That the king is Jewish should be enough to interest you—to find out more. I don't understand why you aren't even curious about him."

I felt my face getting hot. "The best thing about being here in first century Israel is being with you, Shale."

Shale shook her head. "I can't be everything to you. I believe more than this exists, and when we die, we will understand. I hope so, anyway."

She was right. I didn't care about my heritage anymore. I had everything I wanted. Money for my education and the girl I wanted. My special gift helped in lots of ways, too, not the least of which I could get whatever I wanted. Why did I need God?

Shale looked up from her drawing. "Can't you find out where the rabbi is and take me to see him?"

I shook my head. "He's a false prophet, Shale. We've had this discussion many times. If he were a true prophet, he wouldn't cause riots or challenge the Sadducees or Pharisees. They know the Torah better than anyone—including him."

"But Daniel, he's Jewish. He heals people. I mean, you want to be a doctor. And he's a rabbi. When is the last time you even met with a rabbi?"

"When my father was kidnapped."

Shale's face paled. "Is your father dead? You never told me anything about your father."

I turned away. "He was killed by Arabs, we think, on a business trip—extremists."

"Daniel, I'm so sorry." Shale's voice soothed me. She set her drawing aside and leaned into me. "Forgive me for judging you. I didn't know."

"That was the last time I spoke to a rabbi," I said glibly.

Shale scooted on her knees and turned my head towards her. "You should meet this rabbi yourself. Don't waste the opportunity, Daniel. We don't always have second opportunities in life to do the important things. It's too easy to squander what matters most for the sake of convenience. We could make the time."

I shook my head. "No."

Shale looked towards the house. "I must go." She picked up Cherios and her artwork and walked to the gate.

In my mind, I saw Judd and Scylla conferring. Scylla wanted to talk with me.

CHAPTER 25 BETROTHAL

S cylla shut the door and pointed. "Sit here." Her breath reeked of alcohol—her usual condition when Brutus's absences were prolonged. Despite my dislike for her, I pitied the woman.

She crossed her arms and hovered over me. "Shale will be sixteen in a few weeks."

"I know. She told me."

Twisting her hair with her fingers, she spoke with a slur. "You know she is to be betrothed to Judd."

I raised my eyebrows. "Oh, I didn't know," I lied. I only knew from eavesdropping on the private conversations of Judd and Scylla, but I didn't have to tell her that. "Does Shale know this?" I inquired.

Scylla's face paled. "I assume her mother informed her. After all, isn't that why she returned—to honor the contract?"

I shrugged. "She never mentioned it to me."

Scylla turned her head and frowned. That's odd she never mentioned it to you. I was under the impression that she and Judd were already making plans for the betrothal."

"Who told you that?" I asked.

"Why, of course, Judd did." Scylla turned up her nose. "I don't talk to Shale, she's too disrespectful."

I leaned in towards Scylla. "Tell me more about the contract."

Scylla crossed her arms. "The contract was written shortly after Shale's birth. When Shale's mother ran off, Judd's family assumed the contract was broken. They never expected her to honor the agreement."

"I'm familiar with that part of the story," I said impatiently. "I want to know what the contract says."

Scylla laughed. "I'm getting there, my friend." She picked up her wine glass and sipped.

"When Shale returned, Judd struggled. He was in love with another young woman and had no plans to marry Shale. After a while, though, he realized it would be a disgrace not to marry her."

I listened as Scylla explained the details, although her resuscitation of the facts conflicted with what I knew. Judd and Shale were not making any plans to get married—I knew that for sure.

Scylla sat on the bed and looked up at the ceiling. "Judd realizes now he loves Shale, and she is coming of age."

My mind wandered. Judd was not in love with Shale. He only wanted the dowry that came with her—no doubt sizeable. Maybe there wasn't any contract at all—perhaps there was a deal between Judd and Scylla and Scylla would get a kickback if Judd married her. I'd have given anything to see the contract.

I perceived Scylla's thoughts before she spoke. She wanted to work this to her advantage. She had one thing on her mind.

She glided behind the chair. She stroked my head, leaned over, and whispered in my ear, "Do you love Shale?"

"I don't know," I lied.

She slid back around to the front. Her perfume was intoxicating.

"She is a beautiful girl."

"Yes, she is," I agreed.

Scylla leaned forward and spoke in a smooth voice. "I can make you happy. No one would know but you and me."

I shook my head. "No, Scylla."

She persisted. "Brutus is never here. You can stay and help with Nathan. The signs are in the heavens it is to be."

I stopped her from saying more. "Scylla, I respect Brutus too much. You are his wife. Shale will have to decide for herself what she wants. I will respect the contract that was made between the families—many years ago—if there really is a contract."

Scylla looked away disheartened.

I continued. "I have done nothing to bring disgrace to her or the family. If the contract is broken, let it not be because of me."

Scylla's eyes burned.

Nothing is so bitter as unfulfilled desire.

I stood to leave.

"Wait," Scylla said. She touched my shoulder gently. "I can give you more money for your education. You will be without a job. I can make you very happy."

I shook my head. "You can make me happy by never slapping Nathan again."

She backed away from me. "That was the only time it happened."

I approached the door. "Let me say goodbye to him and I'll be on my way."

"Liar! You do love her," she screamed. Scylla threw her drink in my direction. It hit the wall and shattered on the floor.

"Bad aim." I slammed the door behind me.

No sooner had I left than I realized Judd had been listening.

"I'll be sure and send you an invitation to the wedding," he sneered.

I ignored him in disgust.

I walked outside and found Nathan and Mari together in the portico.

I was thankful I wouldn't have to go through the announcement twice. I'd make it simple and addressed both of them. "I'm heading back to Doctor Luke's."

Mari's smile left and Nathan's eyes widened. I leaned over and hugged Nathan. "You've been a good student. I've taught you how to write and you can write out your requests for Mari. She'll be here for you as before."

Mari's countenance fell. "This has to do with Judd, doesn't it?"

I studied the stones on the portico. I had never noticed they alternated between brown and yellow. "Yes, the betrothal to Shale. The only way Shale will grow to love him is if I leave."

Mari shook her head. "Shale will never love Judd. She loves you. A woman can see these things. Her eyes are for you, Daniel."

"Honor is more important than love."

"But there is a catch."

I didn't know about any catches. "What? And how do you know?"

"I've seen the contract."

"So there really is a contract? I'd give anything to see it."

"It's hidden away. I saw it before it was relevant several months ago. For some reason, Scylla had left it out on the table. The next day it was gone." Mari sighed. "It was very one-sided and unfair to the girl, but her mother was desperate for money. That was the first time I knew Brutus even had a daughter."

I shook my head. "Did they pay off her mother or something?"

Mari leaned forward in the chair and whispered. "I don't know the details but there was something scandalous that happened. Brutus acquiesced to keep his good name. I overhead Scylla and Brutus arguing after I saw the contract. Brutus said he never thought Shale's mother would honor the contact—that it was just to get money out of him."

I soaked in Mari's words, trying to understand.

Mari added. "Something must have happened for Shale's mother to send her daughter back here."

I thought about Shale's family background, her mother remarrying, that Shale didn't get along with her stepfather—maybe her mother and stepfather just didn't want her around anymore.

Mari sighed. "Women just don't have any rights when it comes to these things."

I pondered Mari's eyes, so full of compassion for Shale. "Maybe someday women will have more rights," I offered.

Mari looked away deep in thought. "Daniel, I've longed to tell you many things—but I've been afraid. I need this job. I will try to find that contract. You will come back?"

I nodded.

"And Shale—are you going to say goodbye to her?"

"No. I don't like goodbyes. She'll find out soon enough."

Mari offered, "Let me fix you some food to take. It's a long way to Dothan and you'll get hungry."

I agreed. While she prepared a snack, I went to my quarters to get my moneybag. I hoped Judd treated the animals well—for Shale's sake.

I stopped by the cave one last time. After pouring out extra feed and embracing Much-Afraid and Cherios, I returned to the portico. Mari was waiting.

She handed me a bag of figs and nuts and fresh bread she had just baked. "Daniel, night will soon be here. Are you sure you don't want to wait and leave in the morning?"

"I'll be fine," I reassured her.

"Make me a promise."

"What's that?"

"Let Theophilus know you arrived safely when you return to Doctor Luke."

Her request surprised me. Why would I announce my dismissal to the person who had recommended me for the job? How would I explain that I left because Scylla accused me of being involved with an employee's betrothed bride?

I could read her mind to find out why this was so important to her, but I didn't have the energy. I was too depressed and distracted by other things.

My heart longed to see Shale one more time, but I was afraid I would become too emotional. I'd focus on Mari's strange request when I returned to visit Dr. Luke.

I left with her statement ringing in my ears. "I've longed to tell you many things. I will find that contract. Promise me you will return."

CHAPTER 26 THE HEALING

I plodded down the road reminiscing about what could have been. All I had were my earnings and memories that would fade with time.

I wanted to get back to 2015. I should have asked that old woman if she could send me back, but I hadn't seen her in almost a year. I still felt guilt over the one ability she had restored to me. Was it so awful, when I had used it for good?

After all, Shale would soon be married to a man she hated and I'd be forgotten.

I pressed ahead, checking again to make sure I had my money. The shekels would be very valuable when I returned home.

I came upon a large house where a crowd was gathered. Women's wails pierced the air. Many of the visitors and mourners had spilled out into the yard.

A group of Jewish men approached from the south. One of them appeared to be the homeowner, a rich man, perhaps an official from the synagogue because of his clothing. The others following him looked like day laborers or fishermen.

The front door stood ajar and people were entering and leaving. I sneaked into the house unnoticed. Weeping women clutched each other around the room. Shock and disbelief covered their faces and their sadness resonated with my crushed spirit.

For the first time since arriving in Galilee, I felt Jewish blood coursing through my veins. What it meant to suffer as a Jew was never far from my conscience—even though I had taken a more liberal path.

A minute later, the men stormed through the door. One of them exclaimed, "Why all this commotion and weeping? The child isn't dead, she's asleep."

The crowd jeered. Someone mocked, "Who is this man who says she isn't dead?" Other voices taunted him. The crowd had gone amok.

I studied the man who said the young girl was sleeping. He seemed like an ordinary man, not striking in stature or looks. Who was he?

When I tried to intercept his thoughts, something pierced me. I clutched my temple and keeled over. After a few seconds, my head stopped hurting. I leaned over to someone sitting next to me and asked, "Who is that man?"

"Yeshua of Nazareth and his disciples, Peter, James, and John."

The rabbi Shale wanted to meet—such a small request when she meant so much to me. Why didn't I take her to him?

He appeared to be a harmless charlatan, perhaps deluded—except I couldn't explain what had happened. Did he know I was trying to read his mind?

Three of the men who arrived with Yeshua were directing people. The crowd dispersed and the chaos subsided. I studied the rabbi as I walked towards the foyer. Suddenly his eyes met mine. Did he know I was watching him?

Someone tapped me on the shoulder. "Please go outside."

I nodded. I'd wait outside with the others.

An hour passed. All was quiet when the door opened. Yeshua and his followers stepped outside. The rabbi addressed the crowd, "Say nothing about this to anyone."

They took off and disappeared down the road. I went back inside and was surprised to see the young girl eating. Her mother and father and others were rejoicing, calling it a miracle. Everyone was amazed.

Could I believe that she was really raised from the dead? Shock and confusion rattled me. He couldn't have raised her from the dead—could he? That was impossible, even in 2015. The whole event had to have been set up. The girl was sleeping. Maybe the official's term in office was up. This would generate great publicity for his reelection campaign.

I left the house troubled. I'd have a long night to think about it on the way to Jacob's Inn.

CHAPTER 27 NIGHT

I was warned never to travel alone at night. Even the main roads were dark and oftentimes unsafe. Perhaps walking through the forest would be better. I might even be able to shave a few hours off my travel time.

I left the road and followed a narrow footpath down the mountain. I came to another rough-hewn trail. After a short ways on this trail, two well-used footpaths led in opposite directions.

I saw recent animal tracks but did not know what kind of animal had made them. Thick stands of fig, dwarf oak, and hawthorn covered the area. The trail started uphill and then descended, which made for easy travel to the lower valley. The air was humid and fresh at the lower elevation. A small stream percolated nearby and the water murmured down the rocks. Two small waterfalls glimmered in the full moon. A wooden sign with an arrow pointed straight ahead—Robbers Creek.

I had heard of this place—tales of robberies of unsuspecting tourists and murders of wealthy businessmen—but I didn't know the location. I thought it was folklore.

Many stories had been written about strange occurrences in the area. I didn't want to be here. Why had I left the road? The area was soaked in splotches of darkness.

I shuddered. I could spend the night and not let my mind run wild or I could keep traveling and risk whatever monsters crouched in wait—wolves and coyotes were as much a threat as muggers.

I was too tired to keep traveling. I was even too tired to backtrack, which was the wisest thing to do, and climb back up the mountain. The whisperings of the water nearby would help me sleep. I could even swim in the morning.

I made a makeshift bed in the small meadow on the middle ridge. Having some elevation would help me to see any approaching animals. I lay on a bed of leaves, hiding my moneybag underneath me. It couldn't be that much further to Dothan. When light returned, I'd get my bearings.

Even through the tree canopy, the stars burst out in the night sky. The sounds of crickets and the cooing of doves and loons reminded me of days when I was young, the camping trips we took.

Despite my uneasiness, I drifted off. In a dream, fire surrounded me. The flames shot into the air and made a circle, trapping me. My feet were cemented in stone. Smoke filled my lungs and I couldn't wake up.

A creature danced around the fire, but I couldn't see the face. I wasn't sure if it was a man or a woman. The creature turned towards me. The yellowish rotting teeth revealed the dancer's identity. She wore the same clothes she had worn before. The shadows from the fire gave her a hellish appearance.

I awoke with a start. I sat up, checking to make sure I hadn't been robbed. I rubbed my eyes, but the smoke burned. Several feet away a campfire blazed. The old woman sat cross-legged in front of the fire, stoking it with a pitchfork. I waited for my eyes to adjust. I tasted sour stomach contents and swallowed. I wished I had water.

The strange creature was singing a minor key dirge and laughing. Her eyes found me, and she pointed at me with her bony finger. "Come to me," she spoke to my mind.

I shook my head.

"You love campfires. When you were little, you told creepy stories by the fire as you roasted marshmallows. Come join me. The air is cold. Come warm your hands."

I wanted to run away, but I couldn't. Or I was too afraid to move. Maybe she was a demon.

I recalled a conversation with Shale. She saw a dark creature that she called an underling. I cringed. I'd forgotten what Shale told me—until now.

Had I made a pact with the devil? I should kill her. No one would know. I could claim self-defense if anyone ever connected me with her. I could snatch the pitchfork and stab her with it. No one would miss her—especially me.

"Why would you want to kill me?"

Fear seized me. She knew what I was thinking. How dare she—but had she not given me that power? She spoke in a smooth snake-like voice. "Sit with me by the fire."

Who was she? Only a spiritual being could perform magic. She was not an angel.

"Come to me, Daniel. You weren't afraid of me before. Why are you now? Come join me. I have something special to give you."

She stoked the fire with the pitchfork and the fire shot up. Flames swirled around her. How could she not be burned?

"No," I yelled. "Go away. Leave me alone." I shivered.

She laughed. "Why do you want to get rid of me, Daniel? I've made your life so much easier than it would have been. That's why I haven't been around. I didn't need to worry about you going to the dark side. You should thank me."

What did she mean? What did Shale tell me? The woman had sabotaged my thoughts and I couldn't think straight. Why would she show up now?

The demon was cooking fish. My stomach growled.

She stood and started walking towards me with the pitchfork in her left hand.

"Go away," I demanded. "I want nothing to do with you."

"By whose authority do you think you can order me around?" The creature smirked.

"By the power of the living God." In an instant, the bag woman was gone.

I had no idea where the words originated. I hadn't spoken them, but if I didn't, who did?

She had to be a demon. I looked behind her and the fire was out, as if someone had doused it with water.

I clasped my bag and climbed back up the trail. I didn't care how steep the mountain was. I ran as fast as my tired legs could get me off the cursed ground.

That strangely familiar odor reached me as I gulped in the cold night air—the smell of rotten eggs. Every time the woman appeared, the smell was present. Once I reached the desolate, dark road, I hightailed it all night to Dothan and reached the outskirts of the town at dawn. When I saw the sign for the leper colony, I knew I was home. I never thought seeing the sign would bring me such comfort.

CHAPTER 28 SURPRISE MEETING

Several weeks passed since I had arrived in Dothan. The poor and infirm made daily visits to Dr. Luke. Some men and women stopped by just to be encouraged. He worked tirelessly to help everyone. I was surprised I didn't see Simon, the leper, when I made several deliveries to the leper colony. I feared he had died.

Later, Dr. Luke told me, "The traveling rabbi, Yeshua of Nazareth, healed Simon and nine others."

"Did you see him do it?" I asked.

Dr. Luke shook his head. "I didn't see him, but I heard. It was all anyone talked about for a few days. The lepers came from our colony."

"Do you believe the rabbi healed him?"

Dr. Luke said, "I understand they had to appear before the priests before they could enter the temple. Simon was later seen thanking the rabbi and offering a gift. What is more striking is what the little boy of one of the healed lepers said."

"What was that?"

Dr. Luke looked at his plate and stirred his food. "He said the rabbi was the long-awaited Messiah."

I chuckled. "Children are very gullible."

Dr. Luke furrowed his brow.

Did he really believe it might be possible?

"Suppose he is, Daniel?"

I shrugged. "What are the odds? What is the proof?"

Dr. Luke leaned back in his chair and crossed his leg. "Nevertheless, Simon is healed, as well as the others, and I don't know how."

"But you didn't see Simon yourself, did you?"

Dr. Luke thought for a minute. "No, I didn't. He began following Yeshua and sharing his healing with others. I expect him to stop by sometime in the future." Dr. Luke laughed. "A healthy person has no need of a doctor."

I agreed the rabbi was mysterious, but so was the ventriloquist. Israel had a long history of sorcerers, false prophets, and diviners. Even Israel's prophets were not very popular with the people, although I never understood why. I suddenly realized how woefully lacking I was in understanding some of my Jewish history.

I leaned towards the doctor. "It's been four hundred years since God has spoken to us. Why would God send someone now?"

Dr. Luke chewed on my question. "Why not?"

I swallowed hard. I held to my belief that while Yeshua may be a learned rabbi and a good man, that he had to be a false prophet.

"What about the Sanhedrin, Doctor Luke? Is there even one member out of the seventy that takes him seriously?"

Dr. Luke nodded. "Two. Joseph of Arimathea and Nicodemus."

I swallowed hard again. "Oh, I didn't know. Interesting." I suddenly lost my appetite. I could debate this all day and come up with reasons to justify my doubt. Dr. Luke didn't know about the suffering of the Jews for the next two thousand years. Wasn't the Messiah supposed to restore Israel? And Yeshua seemed to spend most of his time attacking the religious leaders and not Rome.

Dr. Luke changed the subject. "I need to go into town today. Would you like to help me bring back the supplies?"

"Sure."

"Great. We'll leave as soon as I check and see what we need."

An hour later we traveled into town. Dr. Luke was frequently stopped by people and he talked with anyone who passed us. Many were former patients. Some were just old time buddies.

I tapped Dr. Luke on the shoulder. "I'm going to stop by and say 'hi' to my sister. I won't be gone long."

Dr. Luke waved me on.

Martha's bright smile greeted me. "Daniel, it's so good to see you again."

I leaned over and hugged her. We laughed and chitchatted about the past. Her business had taken off. "Do you know of anyone who would like a job?" she asked.

I thought about the women I knew. I shook my head. "Maybe I could help you out occasionally," I suggested.

"Like you know anything about women's clothing and accessories," she laughed. "When do you start medical school?"

"Soon. I've been saving my money."

Martha smiled. "Good for you."

She leaned over the counter and whispered to me. "Daniel, I want to tell you something."

What was all the secrecy? "What's that?"

"Do you remember Abbey, my good friend, who had been sick for many years?

I searched my memory for a friend of Martha's from my time, but I couldn't place her.

"She was healed."

"That's great. Is it a secret that you should whisper it?"

"Daniel, have you heard about the rabbi from Nazareth? People are calling him a miracle worker, a great prophet."

My muscles tensed. "Yes, I've heard about him."

Martha whispered, "He healed her."

"What was wrong with her?"

Martha looked embarrassed. "She had female issues. Bleeding. That's why she never married. She couldn't go to the temple because she was always—unclean. Couldn't be around men in that condition. She felt ostracized. She might as well have been a leper. Poor woman. She'd been to every doctor and spent all of her money."

"So what happened?"

"The last time she was in town, I told her to go see Doctor Luke. I knew he wouldn't charge her. Doctor Luke told her about

Yeshua from Nazareth. She went to see him—had to fight the crowds to get near him and managed to touch his robe. That's all it took, just touching his robe. Can you believe it?"

"Sounds like a miracle," I heard myself saying.

"Yes." Martha's eyes sparkled.

"Who do you believe he is?" I asked.

Martha shook her head. "I don't know. I want to meet him. Maybe he'll be in Jerusalem at Passover."

"Yes, maybe."

All the talk about the Jewish rabbi and Messianic claims overwhelmed me. "I must be going. It's good to see you."

We embraced. "Let me know if you need anything."

"Don't stay gone so long next time," Martha chided me.

I found the supplies Dr. Luke wanted and rejoined him a short time later. I hoped I didn't hear another word about Yeshua from Nazareth for a few days.

We were almost to Jacob's Inn when I noticed a familiar face.

"Shale!" I rushed over. "I had a strange feeling I would see you again."

Shale was upbeat, though tired from the journey. Baruch stood behind her. I imagined it was a much quicker journey on a donkey than on foot, but still a long one. I focused my eyes on her face. Did she bring me good news?

Dr. Luke walked up. "Should I know your friend?"

I smiled. "Doctor, this is my friend, Shale, the daughter of Brutus, son of Dirk."

Dr. Luke tipped his head. "How is your brother?"

Shale pounced on his question. "Oh, Doctor Luke, he needs Daniel to return."

Dr. Luke looked concerned. "Is he sick?"

Shale shook her head. "No, he's fine. He misses Daniel terribly."

Dr. Luke turned to me.

I wasn't sure what to say.

The doctor reached over and rubbed my shoulder. "The young lady has traveled a long way on behalf of Brutus's son. You should accompany her back and check on Nathan. The work here will wait until you can return."

Did I want to go back and deal with Scylla and Judd? Only a couple of months had passed. Shale and Judd would be engaged soon.

I nodded. "Yes, Doctor Luke. Of course."

"Give my best to Brutus when you see him."

Shale smiled. "Yes. I will."

Once Dr. Luke had left, I glared at Shale. Some things weren't fixable—things that were written and sealed long ago. Could we alter our future? I didn't want to bargain with fate. I feared I had already bargained with the devil.

Shale interrupted my thoughts. "You can't leave like that, Daniel. Nathan needs you."

I snapped. "I was fired. Doctor Luke doesn't know it."

"Who fired you?"

"Shale, you know Scylla fired me. You think I would have left on my own?"

"She can't fire you," Shale insisted.

I rocked on my heels. "That woman can do whatever she wants."

"She's not my mother."

"She's not my mother either, but that doesn't mean I can do whatever I want."

By now I was yelling and people were staring. A couple of nosy eavesdroppers were listening.

"Let's go around to the back. We can sit at the table and talk." I motioned for Shale to follow me.

A few minutes later we sat across from each other as if we were strangers. I didn't know how to break the tension. I couldn't give Shale what she wanted.

"You shouldn't have come." I looked away to avoid Shale's obvious pain. I hated myself for sounding so insensitive.

"You're treating me rudely."

She didn't have to tell me. What was I becoming? I wasn't being the person I wanted to be. Shale reached over to touch my arm and I flinched.

She bit her lip and tears welled up in her eyes. "Fine. Be that way, while Nathan sits in Nazareth crying his heart out because

143

you're gone and he has no one who understands him, let alone that he can talk to."

"I can't do anything more for Nathan. I taught him how to read and he can write messages."

Shale shook her head. "Guys are all alike—jerks. I thought you were different. It must be that other woman."

I laughed. "Woman? What other woman?"

Shale rolled her eyes. "The one I saw you with when I came into town. You know who I'm talking about."

I shook my head. "No, I don't."

Shale scrunched up the cloth of her dress with her hand over her chest. "I bought this from her when I first arrived from the garden. Martha, she sells feminine things—perfume and such. She has her own booth in town."

I stopped. "You mean my sister?"

Shale stared. "That's your sister—Martha? The one you were having a lively conversation with earlier today? The one you hugged?"

I chuckled. "That's my sister. Back home in my dimension, she runs her own apparel store. Here she does the same thing, though on a much smaller scale. She's my only family here—at least that I have met, except for Mari, though I don't know what our relationship is."

Shale repeated herself. "Martha is your sister?"

I nodded. "Seriously."

Shale's demeanor changed and her face turned red. "I feel foolish."

I wished we could start this whole conversation over.

"Shale, the real reason I left isn't because I'm madly in love with another woman, as you're supposing. When Scylla told me about the betrothal for you to marry Judd, it got complicated."

Shale's eyes searched my face. "How so?"

"You were given to Judd a long time ago. Judd told Scylla I shouldn't be spending so much time with you, even though we were just friends."

Shale remained silent.

"I was afraid I would disgrace you. You are to be betrothed to another man. I couldn't justify it once Scylla told me of the impending marriage."

Shale's eyes flashed. "Are you crazy? I hate Judd, and he's not even from my—world."

I shrugged. "When you're with the Romans, you do as the Romans do."

Shale rolled her eyes. "What's that's supposed to mean?"

"It means you need to follow the rules."

"Daniel—" Shale stopped midsentence.

"What?" I knew where this was going. I pushed my mind reading ability away. I didn't want it anymore.

"The real reason I came for you is different. It wasn't because you left me."

"Why did you come?"

Shale bit her lip. "After you left, I took the animals on a short day trip over the hills. We ran into a man who lived in the cemetery, half-naked, full of demons and…"

"And?" I prompted her.

"Wait, let me back up. The reason we went out for the day was because Judd wasn't feeding the animals. Lowly said he was starving."

"Lowly the pig?"

"Yes. He wanted to go to another farm to get some food. There wasn't any place nearby with pigs."

I nodded.

"Later, a fishing boat pulled up. Cherios said one of the fishermen was the king that I told you about."

I couldn't believe she was telling me another story about the rabbi.

"The lunatic?"

"He's not a lunatic," Shale corrected.

I didn't want to hear anything else about the prophet. "Keep going," I urged her. "Get to your point." I checked behind her to see if anyone was coming.

Shale was irritated at my inattention. "You talk about me being impatient. I traveled on the back of a donkey for hours to get here."

I apologized. "Sorry."

She continued. "The wild man ran straight towards the king—the fisherman. The look in the king's eyes stopped him. Demons left the man and went into the pigs. Then the pigs stampeded into the lake and drowned."

Out of all the stories I had heard, this one was the most bizarre. "You expect me to believe that?"

"Yes," Shale said. "It's true."

I shook my head. "Shale, I've heard similar stories. Gossip travels fast here."

Shale insisted. "It's true."

Who was this man? I couldn't read his mind when I tried. I realized now I feared him. "So what does that have to do with me, or us?"

Shale reached out to me again, placing her hand on my arm. She traced her fingers along the top.

"I want to take Nathan to see the king. If he could heal that cemetery man, he could help Nathan speak."

I shook my head. "No."

"Look," she pleaded, "if the king healed Nathan, he could talk and be normal, right? He's not stupid, is he?"

"No." I leaned on the table, propping up my chin. I didn't want to take him—not because I didn't think he could heal Nathan, but because I was afraid.

"Nothing can heal Nathan. He's been that way since birth."

"What makes you think the king can't heal him?"

"You saw something that you can't explain, but who knows. Maybe the man wasn't crazy. It could have been staged."

Shale frowned. "He tried to attack me on the way over to the farm."

"Maybe that was his test run."

Shale bit her lower lip. "Why do you say such things?"

I shook my head that was now pounding. "Shale, that man you call the king, he's no healer. He's a charlatan. He's nothing."

Shale's voice quivered. "Suppose you're wrong? Are you going to abandon Nathan without trying?"

I didn't know what to do. Even though I didn't want the ventriloquist's gift anymore, I didn't know how to get rid of her influence. Her power was like poison to my soul. After the last encounter I hadn't tried to read anyone's mind. I didn't want to do anything that would make her return.

The power was first given to me by God. Why was I so resistant to the things of God now—or this self-proclaimed rabbi? What if the rabbi could heal Nathan? And I loved Shale, even if I couldn't marry her. Given the choice, would I do the right thing for her brother?

I stood and paced. I felt very small and alone. If only I could pray to God, but I had given up on prayer. Conflicting emotions made me indecisive. I felt like a man drowning. I cried out in spite of myself, "Please help me, God."

No sooner had I said those four words than I felt immediate relief. I walked over to the table.

"All right, Shale. I'll go back with you and find this healer, with one condition."

Shale's eyes popped open. "What's that?"

"No one knows I'm back. And once we've finished our task, proving to you he's—a fraud, I'm coming back to Doctor Luke's."

Shale's excitement waned now that I had agreed. "Do you hate me for doing this?"

"Do I hate you—for goodness' sake, Shale, I don't hate you. You're—so persistent. Even if Judd hadn't been chosen for you, I needed to leave."

"How do you think I felt when I found out you were gone without saying goodbye?"

I met Shale's eyes. "This was arranged long ago. I wanted to appease Scylla. I wish I knew what to do for Nathan."

Shale smiled. "You will come back with me?"

"Yes, with the conditions I gave you."

"Where will you stay?"

I laughed. "Out of sight. You need to find out where that lunatic and his friends are staying. It won't be easy."

A question popped into my head. "How did you get here? I mean what did you tell Scylla?"

"Nothing. I promised Judd a golden nugget for his help."

"With gold? I won't ask where that came from."

She laughed. "I thought you could read my mind."

I shifted my eyes away. I didn't want to use the power again. I'd promised myself that I wouldn't. "I can, but I have to put effort into it. You didn't steal it, did you?"

"Of course not," Shale said indignantly.

If I didn't tell her, she would question my ability. This would be the last time. I'd focused on her thoughts. Never again, I told myself. Now that Shale knew I was trying, she tried to block me— unsuccessfully.

"So you got it from the garden?"

Shale nodded.

"Kol Hakavod. Well done." I was thankful that God revealed the answer to me, unexpectedly, but now Shale seemed distracted. "What are you thinking?"

Shale shrugged. "Nothing. I told Judd to tell Scylla I went to Jerusalem to search for my father. She won't expect me back for a few days."

I started making a mental checklist. "We'll need to sneak Nathan out of the house. That won't be easy. He never goes anywhere."

"We have time, before Judd wants his golden nugget or thinks I've betrayed him."

"Don't worry about him. We've enough to think about just taking care of Nathan. Let's go."

We walked back around to the front of Jacob's Inn to get Baruch, the donkey. I told Shale to wait. "I need to get something from Doctor Luke. I'll be back in a minute."

She reached out and snatched my arm. "Like what, what do you need to do?"

Was she afraid I would leave her again? "Potion, so Scylla will sleep like a baby." I left Shale standing by Baruch.

CHAPTER 29 WANDERINGS

I rummaged through the medicines and found what I needed but Baruch's whinnying interrupted my thoughts. When I went outside, I saw Baruch but Shale was missing.

I searched the front portico, along the street, and checked inside the shops. Scary ideas went through my head. Where was she? I glanced across the walkway. There I saw her standing in the flowerbed. When I reached her, she stood in front of a dancing cobra. His menacing eyes looked ready to strike.

"Shale, give me your hand."

She half-heartily extended it. I tugged. She resisted. The cobra hissed.

"Shale, come to me," I urged. Out of the sky a white dove descended. The movement caught her attention and broke the spell. Shale backed away and collapsed in my arms. I held her tightly as she sobbed.

Several men who had witnessed my distress rushed over. Once they saw the snake slithering away in the grass, they set about to kill the viper. We left them to the task—Shale had been traumatized enough.

We journeyed back to Galilee without much conversation. The solitude gave me time to think. I replayed in my mind all the weird things we had both faced. Were we battling demons?

Perhaps I was as shaken up as Shale. I wouldn't have believed such a thing could happen. Did I still believe honor was more important than love?

I walked beside Baruch, longing to return home, but I didn't know how to make that happen. Shale didn't know how to get back either. Were others stranded in a twilight zone battling demons? Where was God and why hadn't he revealed himself?

We arrived in Nazareth in the early evening and stopped just short of the house. How would we get Nathan out of the house without Scylla knowing?

"Shale, what about that crow that follows you around? Could he create a distraction with Mari, and you sneak in and put the potion in her wine?"

Shale was skeptical. "Mari promised she would do anything for me if I ever needed help. I don't trust Worldly Crow. In fact, I don't trust any crow."

I couldn't argue with her, but whatever we did was going to require creativity or luck—maybe even some divine intervention.

I walked over to a rocky outcropping and sat. My legs burned from so much walking. I studied the potion in the flask and shook it. "We only get one chance. If Scylla catches us, it's all over."

Shale nodded. "Mari cares about Nathan. Knowing we're helping him to be healed will be enough."

I agreed, but I was worried Mari could be persuaded to tell Scylla if confronted. I didn't want her to feel threatened. I also didn't trust Scylla, especially when she drank. I remembered the time she slapped Nathan.

"We need to make sure Scylla doesn't find out that Mari knows anything."

Shale slid off Baruch, walked over, and sat beside me. "As long as we're back by the time Scylla wakes up, everything should be fine."

I leaned back on the ledge stretching my legs. "You know better than me."

Shale turned towards me and smiled. She lingered on my face as if pondering a deep thought. "Do you think we will ever make it back?"

I sighed. "I'm still wondering why we are both here. Why us? Have you met anyone else that's from the future?"

Shale shook her head. "I think God brought us together."

"Why?" I asked. "What's so special about us? Why here? Why you and me?"

Shale leaned back and placed her head on my shoulder. "Maybe when we meet the king, he will give us answers. By the way, did you find out where the king is?"

"Me?" I asked.

"Yes," replied Shale.

I shook my head. "And you mean teacher." I set the flask in the grass and gazed out over the golden field. Sunsets were my favorite part of the day. I didn't know how to say it any other way than to be blunt. "I refuse to call him a king."

Shale shrugged. "How about healer—or rabbi?"

"Rabbi might be better." I was too tired to debate it further. "You better go and ask Mari. I want to get started. I hope God grants us success."

I liked the way that sounded.

Shale stood and brushed the dirt from her dress. "Wish me luck."

"No, not luck. I'll be praying. Don't forget this." I handed her the potion.

"Thanks." A grin crossed Shale's face.

For someone who had rejected God, freedom washed over me unexpectedly. Why had I waited? I should pray before I talked myself out of it.

I closed my eyes. "Grant us success in helping Nathan to be healed."

My first prayer in two years. How long would I feel this way? Maybe it was the moment, watching the sunset, Shale's presence beside me once again, admiring the fertile valley. The golden hues of the field had darkened. Clouds drifted by in a mass of swirling reds beneath the setting sun, as if a great artist had left his imprint on the sky.

I was excited and afraid. Would we be able to find the rabbi? I lay on my back, closed my eyes, and dozed.

It seemed only minutes later that I heard footsteps. When I looked up, I saw Shale.

"We're all set," she said excitedly.

"You gave Mari the potion?"

"Yes, she was fine with it. It was easier than I thought it would be."

"Great. Now that we've taken care of that, where are we going?"

Shale's countenance fell. "You didn't find out?"

I shook my head. "I didn't have time to think about it. I assumed you knew. I found the potion and then became distracted with you and that cobra."

Shale bit her lip. "I have no idea where the king is."

I had just prayed and now we didn't even know where to go. "I thought you had this figured out. This was your idea."

Shale remained quiet, although I could tell she was disheartened. She sat beside me and put her head on my shoulder. "Daniel, it seems more natural for you to ask the men than for me."

I didn't have any answers though I liked her being close to me. Then she stood and walked over to Baruch, sat on the log, and crossed her arms.

We stared at each other in silence.

I heard Much-Afraid's yelps first. She ran over and greeted us.

"How did you get here?" Shale asked the dog. She scratched Much-Afraid behind the ear.

Darkness would arrive soon. We needed to know what to do. I tried not to sound too critical. "Why didn't you ask me earlier?"

"I did," Shale quipped.

"No, you didn't."

A couple of minutes passed. It was too late to go into town and ask.

Shale's eyes focused on something. I turned. A sheep approached from the nearby field.

Why would a sheep be walking all alone? "I should take it back over to the field—to the other sheep." I stood.

Shale said, "No, wait."

"Why?"

She held up her hand for me to be quiet. "The sheep is talking to me."

Then the sheep walked back across the street to rejoin the herd.

"Don't tell me you were talking to that animal."

"But I was," Shale said.

"How can you do that? I didn't hear anything."

"Like you can talk to Nathan and I can't."

I stared at the ground. Shale's ability wasn't tainted like mine. I remained silent, wishing I were as good a person as she thought I was. She would be devastated if she knew the truth.

"So what did the sheep tell you?"

"You know."

I wasn't going to call on the medium. The more I used it, the more it controlled me. Should I confess to Shale that I was a fraud? My ability to read minds was wicked and wrong now. Even though it started out as something good, I had substituted a counterfeit.

I felt a strong sense of a supernatural presence. Perhaps I should pray. I closed my eyes. "Abba Father, you once helped me to read minds. Tell me where we are to find this man Shale believes is a king."

Nothing happened. I prayed again, this time more fervently. "Please, show us the way." Suddenly, the words appeared in my mind—miraculously.

"We're to go to the Decapolis area," I said.

Shale nodded.

How did that happen? I glanced up at the darkened sky.

Shale interrupted my thoughts. "Let's not wait until the morning. I want to go back to the house to listen now."

"I'll stay here with Baruch. Take Much-Afraid with you."

Shale slapped her thighs urging Much-Afraid to follow her. "Come on, you can keep me company while I wait."

CHAPTER 30 DECAPOLIS

I t seemed only minutes later when I heard Shale's voice. For a moment, I had forgotten where I was. How long had I slept? The moon had moved across the sky.

"Scylla is asleep. Let's get Nathan now," she whispered.

"Great," I mumbled. "Let me sleep a little longer." I turned over on my other side.

"No, I don't want to wait. Let's go now. Who knows how long the sedative will last."

I willed my eyes to open. "Right now?"

"Yes." Shale's insistence jarred me. I sat up and rubbed my eyes. It seemed strange to be out in the field at night kidnapping Shale's brother from a place I used to call home.

Sleep deprivation made me see things differently. It seemed too risky. Why had I agreed? Did I really believe it would make any difference to Nathan? He'd never been able to speak.

I glanced at Shale who was so wide-eyed I was annoyed. She stood in my shadow with her hands on her waist.

I motioned for her to back up. "Give me some space, okay?" At least I was sitting. "Are you sure you want to do this?"

Her white teeth glistened in the moonlight. "Of course I'm sure, and the sooner the better. Imagine what Nathan's life would be like if the king—I mean, the rabbi—healed him. And he'll be so thrilled to see you. Please get up."

"Okay. Give me a second." I stood and stretched my back and arms, and rubbed my eyes. My contacts were bothering me again, but I was afraid to take them out in the dark.

"Let's go."

"Should we take Baruch with us to the house?" Shale asked.

"No, he might make too much noise."

Shale told him we'd be back shortly. "And you, too, Much-Afraid, stay here with Baruch."

The dog lay down beside Baruch.

I rubbed my hands to warm them. Hot chocolate would have tasted good right now. We arrived in front of the house a few minutes later.

"Well, here we are," Shale said, stating the obvious.

"Are you sure she's asleep?" I didn't want to run into Scylla in the hallway.

"I heard Mari singing and I'm sure she doesn't sing in the middle of the night."

I walked around to the back and tried to open the door, but the latch was either stuck or locked. I didn't want to bang on it. I tried it again. This time the door moved.

Once inside, I snuck into Nathan's darkened room. I hated to disturb him. I waited for my eyes to adjust.

Then I crept over to his bed, feeling my way so as not to trip over anything. A flashlight would have been nice. When I knelt in front of him, I could hear his restful breathing.

I gently shook him on the shoulder. "Nathan, it's me, Daniel."

He grunted, but didn't move.

"Nathan, it's Daniel."

His eyes popped open. When he saw me, he smiled.

I put my finger over his mouth. "Shush." He couldn't talk, but he could make noises.

I was surprised I could read his thoughts.

"Shale is out front. We want to sneak you out of the house and take you to a rabbi. Shale believes he can loosen your tongue. Would you like to be able to talk?"

Nathan nodded eagerly.

"We don't want to wake up Scylla. She would worry."

He nodded again.

I helped him out of bed.

"Be quiet," I cautioned.

He needed to change into something warmer. "Where are your clothes?"

He pointed to the corner.

"Good. Do it quickly."

While he changed, I made sure everything looked clear.

"Shush," I whispered.

His thoughts told me he was nervous.

"Don't be afraid." He'd never traveled far from home. I didn't know if he had ever been anywhere after dark.

After we left through the front door, I hurried him along. My heart felt as if it would thump through my chest. Leaving the house, knowing the most dangerous part was over, gave me an unexpected buzz.

Shale appeared from behind some bushes.

No sooner had we reached the street than I heard a crow screeching.

"We're going to see the king," Shale said. "Shush."

"Your favorite crow?" I asked.

Shale nodded.

I shrugged. We headed back to where we had left the animals.

Shale took a moment to hug Much-Afraid good-bye. "Go to the house and wait for us to return."

The dog whimpered. I felt sorry for her, but she couldn't go with us.

Shale patted Much-Afraid on the head. "We won't be gone long."

The dog yelped and ran back to the house, her tail bobbing as she crossed the field.

How nice it would be if we could all talk to animals, but if the animals argued, like kids, maybe it wouldn't be good.

I turned to other matters as I prepared Baruch for the journey. Soon we were ready and I lifted Nathan and Shale on Baruch's back.

We traveled through Galilee in the darkness but daylight would arrive soon. I'd check occasionally to see how Shale and

157

Nathan were doing. I caught Shale slouched over Nathan. At least Nathan and I caught a few hours' sleep earlier—Shale didn't get any.

We entered the Decapolis area and arrived on the shore of the Sea of Galilee mid-morning. Crowds had already gathered on the hillside. The lay of the land made it a natural amphitheater.

Now that we were here, I was glad we had brought Nathan— as long as I didn't have to get too close to the rabbi. I'd hang out at the back of the crowd.

I argued with myself. Why was I afraid of him if he were a false prophet? I also feared the ventriloquist. Had I made a pact with the devil? I didn't know where I stood with God.

I was glad for Shale, that she had found a person to fill her spiritual needs. Maybe Yeshua was a good man, even a religious man, but what about the Jews? Would Yeshua be for the Jews also?

Shale jarred me out of my musings. "We'll need to leave Baruch here and walk down."

Shale and Baruch were talking. Some people stared. I pretended I didn't know the young woman.

When Shale finished tethering Baruch, I guided her and Nathan down the mountain. The rabbi's popularity had grown and it was difficult to catch a glimpse of him.

"I see him," Shale said excitedly. She pointed to the rabbi.

"Do you want to take Nathan? I don't want to go any closer."

"Why not?"

How could I explain my doubts about his identity? I kept it simple. "I just don't want to go any closer."

Shale clutched my hand. "You must lead us," she said. "You are head of the household, the oldest. You must go with us."

I relented despite my misgivings. We picked our way through the crowd, careful not to step on the small children. The scene reminded me of the summer concerts in the park in Jerusalem in 2015.

Fear gripped me—I began to think of reasons why we shouldn't ask the rabbi to heal Nathan. Perhaps it was the wrong time. The crowds were waiting patiently for the teacher to speak.

One of Yeshua's followers came up and asked, "What do you need?"

"We have a young mute man who needs to be healed," I said.

The man waved his hand at the crowds amassed on the hill. "The Master is busy. Can't you see?"

I imagined his day filled with curious onlookers and naysayers following him everywhere, making demands on his time. I was exhausted thinking about it.

Shale spoke up. "Please, let us take Nathan to the healer. We have come a long way."

It appeared as though the rabbi heard Shale, even though he was a good distance from us.

Shale continued, "If the teacher could touch Nathan, I know he would heal him."

The rabbi's assistant nodded. "Wait here," he said. He left to speak to him.

A couple of minutes later, the healer approached us. Yeshua's eyes showed tenderness. "Peace be with you."

Shale responded, "And to you, too, Master."

The rabbi smiled. "Follow me."

We left the crowds and he led us to a secluded spot. I lagged, still nervous. The rabbi motioned for Nathan to sit. Nathan sat on a flat rock in front of him. Great anticipation covered the boy's face.

The face of Yeshua was different from anyone I had met. He didn't strike me as a lunatic or a fraud. He didn't seem impressed with his popularity—or lack of. Some people appeared to oppose him, but he seemed not to care.

The rabbi said a Hebrew prayer, spat into his hand, and touched Nathan's tongue. Looking up to heaven, he cried, "Ephphatha!"

Nathan opened his mouth wide and moved his tongue. Once he realized he could speak, his eyes grew bright. He laughed as if surprised by joy.

Nathan dropped to his knees before the rabbi. "Thank you, my Lord."

I stared at the healer—mystified by what I had just witnessed.

Yeshua acknowledged the boy's thankfulness.

159

Nathan turned to the crowd that had followed us. They wanted to see the miracle the rabbi had performed.

"I can speak! I can speak! Hear me." Nathan took hold of my cloak and yanked on it. "Daniel, can you hear me?"

I laughed. "Yes, Nathan, I can hear you."

He went over and bowed before the king once more. "Thank you, my Lord."

The rabbi said to him, "When you leave, don't tell anyone what I've done."

The crowds stared in amazement. Many shook their heads.

Shale ran over and hugged Nathan, tears in her eyes.

She faced the rabbi. "Thank you for healing my brother."

Yeshua smiled.

Others asked, "Who is this man that does such miracles? Where does he come from?"

"He comes from Nazareth," a woman replied.

"Nazareth—can anything good come from there?"

Division mounted among the crowds. I wasn't the only one with unanswered questions.

Unexpectedly, Yeshua looked at me.

I glanced away. His eyes were all knowing, making me feel uncomfortable. I forced myself to look back at him—and meet his gaze.

"Thank you," I said in my mind, "for healing Nathan."

The rabbi's eyes looked beyond my uncertainty. I suddenly realized he was looking at me like he knew me—really knew me. Not even like my own family. Was he clairvoyant? And why did I feel so emotional? There was either something totally real about this man or this was an incredible case of mass hypnosis. I didn't know which.

All I knew was this was more than about reading minds. He could read mine like he'd been doing it for years. Surely he was more than a man, more than a teacher, more than a healer, and more than a rabbi. Who was he?

Some Jews still waited for the Messiah. Others identified Yeshua as the Messiah. Could the Jews have been wrong for the last two thousand years? My skepticism wouldn't let me go that far.

160

I would search the Hebrew Scriptures to see if they said anything about this man named Yeshua. There must be prophecies about a coming Messiah. I wanted to know more. I knew Yeshua was mentioned in the Christian Bible in 2015, but I knew nothing about him appearing in the Torah or Tanakh—then or now.

My musings turned to Nathan. He walked among the crowds sharing his healing. Some wanted to touch him. Others wanted to hear every word he uttered.

I overheard one man commenting, "He even makes the deaf hear and the mute speak."

Some doubted. "I bet he could talk all along," another man said. "Someone who has never talked couldn't talk as well as he can."

I saw myself in him, refusing to believe because it was too hard to believe in miracles.

A short while later, the rabbi fetched a small boat and paddled a short distance away from the shoreline. The crowd became quiet as Yeshua began to teach. When had I heard a rabbi speak with such passion and authority? His calm presence was reassuring. I sat by Shale and listened, my curiosity piqued.

Yeshua told a story. "The kingdom of heaven is like a man who sowed good seed in his field; but while people were sleeping, his enemy came and sowed weeds among the wheat, then went away.

"When the wheat sprouted and formed heads of grain, the weeds also appeared.

"The owner's servants came to him and said, 'Sir, didn't you sow good seed in your field? Where have the weeds come from?'

"He answered, 'An enemy has done this.'

"The servants asked him, 'Then do you want us to go and pull them up?'

"But he said, 'No, because if you pull up the weeds, you might uproot some of the wheat at the same time. Let them both grow together until the harvest; and at harvest time I will tell the reapers to collect the weeds first and tie them in bundles to be burned, but to gather the wheat into my barn.'"

Murmurings reached me through the crowds. I overheard some of his disciples discussing the point of the story. I glanced at Shale—did she understand more than I did? I didn't think the story was really meant to be about a farmer dealing with weeds.

The rabbi was different from my preconceived notions—he seemed more Jewish than Gentile and surely the Sanhedrin wouldn't be upset about such simplistic stories as these—there must be more. Besides, I had just witnessed Nathan's healing. Perhaps I had the wrong impression about this rabbi.

Regardless, my curious was piqued. I would have to search the Tanakh and learn what the Hebrew Scriptures said. Brutus had many scrolls I could examine to find out more. What were the Messianic predictions? I was ashamed to admit that I didn't know.

After a while, I realized we needed to return home. I tracked down Nathan and Shale in a small group of Gentiles who were searching for answers to Nathan's healing and wrapped my arm around Nathan. "We need to head back."

We'd almost made it back up the hill when Shale stopped to speak to someone. I waited, but time was passing.

"Shale, come on," I called to her. She waved back. I gave Baruch some fresh water and oats.

Nathan asked me, "When do you think my father will be back in town?"

I shrugged. "I don't know, but we need to send word to him about your miraculous healing."

"What do your writings say about Yeshua?" Nathan asked.

"The rabbi?"

"Yes." The boy's eyes were wide.

"I don't know. Maybe I should find out."

"Being Jewish you must be curious."

I smiled and gave Baruch some water. "Yes, I am."

At last, we were traveling back home. Shale was quiet.

"Are you okay?" I asked.

"Yes," she replied.

I glanced at her face. She looked exhausted. Her eyes were half- closed.

"He's the king above all kings," she stated dreamily.

"You think so?"

Shale became defensive. "And you don't?"

That wasn't what I meant. "I don't know what to think."

We headed down the road not saying anything else.

Soon we had a visitor. Worldly Crow landed on a palm tree as we passed by. I heard Shale saying, "He didn't learn, Worldly Crow."

"What's that?" I asked.

"Oh, nothing. Worldly Crow called the healer a magician."

I grinned. "That's a thought."

Shale asked Nathan. "What's the first thing you're going to say to Scylla when we return?"

"I'm not going to say anything," he whispered.

"What? Tell me you are kidding. You're healed and you're not going to share with others what the king did for you?"

Now it sounded like a brother and sister going at it. While I didn't like the cross words, the sibling rivalry seemed refreshing.

"Didn't he tell me not to tell anyone?"

Shale rolled her eyes. "I don't think that's what he meant, Nathan."

"What did he mean when he told me not to tell anyone?"

Shale shrugged. "I don't know. Maybe don't tell people until they are ready to listen."

"I want my father to hear me first."

Shale was indignant. "You mean, we brought you all the way out here and you aren't even going to speak to Scylla?"

Shale's anger probably had more to do with her dislike of Scylla than wanting to get even with her.

"Besides," Nathan continued, "I want Daniel to remain with us and not leave. That won't happen if Scylla knows I can talk."

Nathan needed a man-to-man talk. His impairment had made him self-centered—a form of self-preservation. He would have to learn the world didn't revolve around him.

I spoke as gently as I could to avoid hurting his feelings. "Nathan, you can't manipulate people. I go where I want. No one controls me, not even you."

Worldly Crow squawked from a tree.

Shale responded, "What do you know about anything, Worldly Crow? Go away. Let me be."

For once, I didn't envy her ability to talk to animals.

CHAPTER 31 COMPLICATIONS

W e returned in the late afternoon. I was anxious to get away, but as we approached, Shale begged me to put Baruch in the cave.

"If you'll take Baruch, I'll sneak Nathan in the house through the portico."

"It's late, Shale. Suppose Scylla sees me?"

"We can make up something."

"We?" I repeated. "I'm not even supposed to be here."

"I'll prevent her from walking outside until you're gone."

Shale was tired and clingy, though I had to admire her. I didn't think I could have stayed awake that long. I suspected the real reason she asked me to take Baruch was because she didn't want me to leave.

If Nathan spoke, he could impress Scylla and then what could she say? Perhaps it made sense. Change is hard, even when it's good. Given time, I was sure Nathan would overcome his fear and stand up to Scylla as a man. She had mistreated him for years.

I stopped short of the gate under the palm trees, where Baruch preferred. Nathan climbed down from the donkey first.

"I couldn't believe all the signs I could read," he said, for the third or fourth time.

I grinned. "You're a good student."

He shook his head. "No, you're a gifted teacher."

Shale dismounted from her donkey and clasped my arm. "Thank you, Daniel, for coming."

I hugged her. The next time I saw her, she might be married.

"Wait here and let me put Baruch in the back."

"No, it's okay." She yawned and rubbed her head. "I want to go with you."

Much-Afraid, wagging her tail, ran up to Shale.

"See, I told you, we wouldn't be gone long," she said.

Cherios hopped out of the cave and found us.

Shale laughed. "Both of you go back inside the cave. I need to say goodbye to Daniel."

The animals obeyed Shale and the moment had come that I needed to leave. I was glad we had a few moments alone after such a dramatic day.

Shale wrapped her arms around me in a warm embrace and I clasped her tightly. I desperately longed to kiss her but knew that I shouldn't.

"Someday we'll be back in our own time period together—I just know it," Shale stated.

I hugged her tighter. "I hope you are right."

After a moment, Shale stepped back and gently brushed her finger down my chest. Her eyes appeared watery. "Can I ask you something kind of personal?

"What's that?"

Shale bit her lip. "Do you have a girlfriend?"

"You mean back home in 2015?"

Shale nodded.

I laughed. "No, I don't."

Shale relaxed at that revelation. She bit her lip again. "Do you feel that I'm too young for you?"

I shook my head and said tenderly, "No."

She leaned against me and whispered, "If you get back before I do, will you look for me? I mean, can we at least be friends on Facebook, or something like that?"

I pulled her close. "I'd want to be more than just Facebook friends. I know it seems impossible now but there is a lot we don't understand—especially about the betrothal and how that might affect the future from which we come."

Shale nodded. "I know."

"We'll just have to wait and see," I reassured her. "But I really care about you."

"Thanks for coming with us today and making this happen."

"I'm glad you convinced me, Shale. We did a good thing."

Shale glanced towards the cave. "I guess I better let you get back to Doctor Luke."

We held hands for the first time as we crossed the veranda in the portico where we met up with Nathan. Suddenly Scylla appeared and her mouth dropped. Her gaze went from me to Nathan to Shale and then back to me. We let go of each other, putting some distance between us. I then realized Judd had been watching us all along—hiding.

"This isn't going to be good," Nathan said.

I touched Nathan on the arm. "Let me take you inside."

He nodded.

Nathan caused me the greatest concern. Shale could deal with Scylla. Bullying by others had made her strong and her new faith would temper her compulsiveness.

Someday she would make Judd a fine wife. I hoped she understood that honor was more important than love. I'd tear up the contract and throw it in the fire if I could.

I shut the door behind us. "Give me a moment outside with Scylla and Shale. It's unfair to Shale. I have as much to do with this as she does. I'll say goodbye before I leave. Do you understand?"

Nathan nodded.

Once outside, steam from Scylla's fiery temper covered the portico—nothing like the wrath of an angry woman. Still I pitied Scylla because she was so disturbed, treating Shale as her own whipping bag.

"Lock her up in her private quarters," Scylla demanded.

Judd didn't move.

"Now," Scylla insisted.

I heard a door slam. Nathan stood behind me. "Wait."

Did he change his mind?

Scylla covered her mouth in shock. "You— you can talk."

"Yes."

Nathan looked as if he'd grown two inches taller. "You're a greedy, jealous woman and the worst example of a stepmother who ever lived. You don't care about me or Shale."

Scylla glared. "That's not true."

"Be quiet," Nathan demanded.

Worldly Crow sat in a nearby tree, squawking.

Nathan continued. "Do you know what it's like to be mute?"

I didn't remember ever seeing Scylla speechless.

Nathan turned towards me. "You've been my friend for the last two years. I love you, Daniel."

I whispered back so no one else could hear, "I love you, too, Nathan."

"But how can you deny what the king did for me?"

I shook my head. "I'm not denying what he did. He performs amazing miracles, is a gifted teacher, and the most impressive rabbi I have ever met, but to call him the Messiah—what proof is there of that?"

Nathan shook his head in my direction, as if discouraged at my response, but then turned his attention to Judd. "You're wicked."

I cringed. Must he be so honest?

"Who made you the man of the house?" crooned Scylla.

Nathan ignored her question. "I want my father to come home."

Scylla stomped her foot in defiance. "No."

"Why not?" Nathan asked. "So you can continue to torture and control the rest of us?"

This was becoming too personal. Now I worried if Judd would lie for Scylla. She could put me in jail for life. I needed to teach Nathan some social etiquette, what not to say, before he dug too many graves.

"I'll leave. This is a family matter," I said.

"No," Shale pleaded. "If you care anything about me—"

Desperation covered her face. I didn't know what to do.

The sky darkened.

I acquiesced. "Maybe Shale is right."

"We don't need you anymore, Daniel," Scylla retorted.

Nathan spoke up. "Even though I can talk, I don't want Daniel to leave."

"He's no longer needed unless you want to waste your inheritance," Scylla fumed.

"Mine or yours?" Nathan asked.

Scylla glared.

Nathan continued. "You've made my father weak, belittled him. You married him for his money."

"No, I didn't," insisted Scylla. "It was foretold in the stars."

Ignoring her retort, Nathan took a couple steps closer. "You've lied repeatedly. What Judd said to you isn't what you told Shale."

"So the truth comes out," Shale scoffed.

Judd stepped back. I reached over and touched Nathan's shoulder.

Scylla turned from Nathan and leaned into Judd. "I told you to take Shale to her room. Lock her up. I'll speak to you later."

Then she focused on Nathan. "You might not be mute but you're still dumb. You don't know what you're talking about."

What an insult to Nathan. Now I was angry. Did she really think Nathan was dumb?

Judd shoved Shale from behind. I wanted to punch him in the stomach. Shale had earned my respect. No matter what happened, she would survive. I had to figure out a way to get us both back to the twenty-first century before she married Judd.

The door slammed behind them and Nathan and I were alone with Scylla.

"We wanted to help Nathan," I said. "Now that he's healed, he can live a normal life. Like the rest of us. Maybe he's too blunt, but with time, he'll learn more self-control."

"I want to see my father," Nathan said. "Can you take me to him?"

Scylla shook her head. "That rabbi has stirred things up so much I don't know that it's safe to travel." Scylla sighed. "We don't need Daniel anymore to help you."

Her eyes turned to me and I felt uncomfortable.

I chose my words carefully. "You know, I could take Nathan to his father."

Nathan jumped at the opportunity. "Could you?"

Scylla hesitated.

How could Scylla justify keeping him here? I wasn't going to meet Scylla's romantic needs, and who knew when Brutus would return. As long as Mari was here—I wasn't willing to leave without Mari staying.

Scylla nodded. "I'll be back in a minute." She went into the house.

Nathan smiled.

Maybe God did care. Where would I find Brutus?

CHAPTER 32 CAESAREA

"Get packed before Scylla changes her mind," I urged Nathan. "One change of clothes is enough."

Nathan bolted towards the door and quipped, "I never thought I'd be able to speak. The king must be a man of God."

I nodded.

He disappeared in the house and Mari caught my eye through the window. I waved for her to come outside.

She hesitated before cracking the door.

"Come here—hurry," I whispered.

Mari eased the door shut and smiled. "I heard Nathan speak for the first time."

She wrapped her arms around me joyfully. "I always believed the rabbi could heal him."

Only Jews referred to him as a rabbi. She must have overheard some Jewish women discussing him in town.

Mari smiled. "I'm so glad for Nathan's sake—and so sorry Scylla doesn't see the blessing."

"You and me, too."

Mari thought for a moment. "If you take Nathan to his father, Scylla may not keep me employed."

"As long as Shale is here, she needs you."

"I suppose."

"You must stay with Shale until I return. Otherwise, I'm going to worry myself sick about her."

"When will you be back?"

"I don't know, but I will be back—even if I must watch Shale wed someone else."

Mari crossed her arms. "Daniel, she loves you. Her eyes are for you."

I remembered she had briefly seen the contract. "Can you remember what the contract says?"

Mari leaned over and whispered. "I searched for the contract while Scylla was drugged last night and found it. There is one contingency."

"Hurry," I whispered. I kept my eyes on the door.

"If Shale meets someone she wants to marry before the betrothal, she can break the contract. Her mother wanted to make sure she wed."

"So Scylla must not have told Shale she had a choice."

"Scylla never talks to Shale unless it is to ridicule her. I don't think Shale knows." Mari turned and looked away. "It's a disgrace for a woman not to wed."

Was Mari talking about herself? "You have many years."

"I was raised by Gentiles, but they kept my identity hidden."

"So you are Jewish?"

Mari nodded.

"Who raised you?"

"Theophilus."

"Theophilus?" No wonder there was this strong connection between Mari and the wealthy Roman.

"Don't say anything to anyone. It's better," Mari cautioned.

"All right." Why wasn't Mari telling me everything?

She interrupted my thoughts. "There is something else."

"What's that?"

At that moment, the door opened. Scylla handed me a scroll. "Brutus's address—where he lives, with his other wife."

What? Did I hear her right?

Scylla went back inside without saying another word.

"With his other wife," I repeated.

Mari's mouth gaped.

"Did you know?" I asked.

"No."

What other family secrets did I not know? "Well, I suppose it won't make any difference with Nathan, except to destroy his image of the perfect father." No wonder Scylla was so bitter. How many women had he been involved with?

"Poor woman," Mari empathized.

"This says Caesarea—I thought he was in Jerusalem."

"If you leave soon, you can arrive before nightfall."

I looked across the field. The sun was still high, but I was exhausted—physically and emotionally. Scylla's constant flirting made sense now. She had everything any woman could want—except love.

I leaned against the post as I debated whether to probe deeper. "How did Scylla meet Brutus?"

Mari's countenance fell. "Oh, that's very dark."

I remembered Scylla's veiled reference to fortunetelling but was curious if Mari knew more.

The young woman wistfully glanced around to make sure no one heard. "A friend took Brutus to Scylla for—advice. She was a mystic. That's all I feel comfortable saying."

I nodded, noting Mari tended to minimize things she found difficult to discuss.

She smiled. "He's still a good man—don't you think?"

I grimaced. Mari would go to great lengths to avoid talking badly about anyone. "Can you tell Nathan to hurry? I want to leave before Scylla changes her mind."

"All right."

"And don't tell Shale about—the other woman."

"I won't," Mari said. "Nathan might when he finds out."

"Let it be from him and not us."

Mari reached over and tapped my arm. "I have something else to tell you."

"What's that?"

She shook her head. "No. I changed my mind. Later." She walked over and clutched the door.

"Can you tell Shale she doesn't have to marry Judd?" I asked quickly.

Mari entered the house before replying.

Why did she say that and then refuse to tell me? Why didn't she respond to my request? She must not have heard me. Should I follow her inside? Suppose Scylla overheard us—I knew she wanted Judd to marry Shale. I still suspected financial gain for Scylla. Why else would she have revealed the contract to Judd?

Frustrated about the lack of answers, I wandered back to the cave. I was surprised to see Judd sitting by the water bin with his hand submerged in the water.

"What are you doing?"

"I burned my hand."

"Oh." I tried to see but he pulled his hand away.

I shrugged. "You'll be glad to know Nathan and I are leaving."

"Oh."

"Shale will make you a fine wife."

"Thank you," he said smugly.

If only there were a way to prevent it—would Mari tell her? Or would Mari get in trouble if she did anything to prevent it?

I sighed. Again, too many unanswered questions. I patted Baruch on the head, hugged the rabbit, and said goodbye to Much-Afraid. Shale's affection for them had rubbed off on me.

"Take care of the animals."

"I always do. They haven't died."

"And don't forget about Lowly."

"Lowly?"

"The pig. That's what Shale named him."

"It's no big deal to me. I'm not Jewish."

Was that meant to be a jab? I let it go. No reason to leave on bad terms.

I found Nathan waiting by the gate. "Ready?"

He nodded.

Mari rushed over and handed Nathan a bag of fruit and fresh bread. "You don't want to go hungry." She turned to me, "Stay safe."

I thanked her. We closed the gate behind us. Nathan was excited to leave, but I felt conflicted. How would I live without Shale? Did she know she could get out of the contract? Perhaps she wasn't told because someone didn't want her to know. Who would benefit by not telling her? I still had this deep-seated feeling that Judd and Scylla had an arrangement, and for some reason, Brutus didn't want to get involved. Perhaps Shale's father was just too preoccupied with his other life outside of Galilee.

Besides all the questions, my heart ached. What good was all the money in the world if I didn't have Shale with me and couldn't get back to 2015?

Despite my bleak outlook, the rolling hills on the way to Caesarea from Nazareth lifted my spirits. Nathan delighted in the magnificent vistas, seeing the many shepherd boys guarding the sheep, and meeting other wayfaring travelers. I hoped he could keep that childlike quality—enjoying the simple things many ignored.

We arrived at Caesarea before sundown. I looked forward to seeing the city in the daylight. Herod had made the city a vacation spot. On every corner, magnificent buildings stood that in modern times lay in ruins. Caesarea was like the Roman capital of Palestine. Many Gentiles lived here year round.

As we neared the center of town, Nathan asked, "After you drop me off at my father's, where are you going?"

I shrugged. "Maybe I'll visit Jerusalem. Go back to Dothan and help Doctor Luke. I don't know."

I asked a street vender for directions to Brutus's flat.

"Very nice area," the man remarked. "All the government officials live on that road. In fact, Pontius Pilate lives nearby when he isn't in Jerusalem."

"Pontius Pilate?"

"Yeah, the prefect. Somebody has to keep order in Jerusalem." He laughed. When I didn't laugh back, he continued. "You go down this road, take a left at the bend, and go a little further. You will come to this street. It's close to the shopping district."

I thanked the man.

The road had lots of foot and animal traffic—a diversity of people, but it seemed as if more Greeks lived here than Jews. I looked forward to seeing the manmade harbor, a magnificent achievement.

We entered the gates of Caesarea and soon came to a two-story villa. It matched the address on Scylla's note. My thoughts returned to Nathan. I hadn't told him that his father had another wife.

"Are you ready?"

He nodded.

We walked up the stone steps and knocked.

Brutus appeared at the door. His eyes went from surprise to joy. "Nathan—what are you doing here?"

"Father!" Nathan cried.

Brutus embraced Nathan warmly—a sweet moment. He motioned for us to follow him. We walked past the kitchen-like area where a woman in a colorful robe was cooking. The delicious smell made my stomach growl. Brutus pointed us to a large living area decorated with Greek and Roman wall hangings and Egyptian rugs.

"Sit down," he said. "Nathan, tell me what happened, how can you speak now?"

Nathan told Brutus how the king had healed him. His father let him talk, nodding occasionally and smiling. Brutus seemed sincere and genuine despite my doubts.

After a few minutes and getting past the shock of hearing Nathan talk, he turned to me. "How is Shale?"

I hesitated. "She's doing well. Wishes you would come home."

"Yeah, I know." He called to the woman in an unfamiliar language.

She brought water for Nathan and me. The woman had dark complexion with exotic features. I couldn't place her ethnicity.

Brutus spoke in Greek and another language I didn't recognize. "This is Nathan and this is Daniel."

The woman smiled and curtsied.

An awkward silence followed.

Then Brutus said, "This is my wife, Lydia."

Lydia smiled.

Nathan turned to his father. "She is your wife?"

"Yes, my wife."

"Scylla isn't your wife?"

"Yes, she is my wife, too."

"So you have two wives?"

"Yes. I have—two—wives."

I glanced at Lydia. She continued to smile.

"Does she know I'm your son?" Nathan asked.

"Oh, yes. She knows," Brutus reassured Nathan.

Brutus had not spoken in the other language again, but kept to Greek.

Soon Lydia went back in the kitchen and finished preparing the food. A short while later, the woman served us a delicious meal. Their hospitality was warm and Nathan and Brutus dominated the meal with nonstop chatter. The woman never said anything but smiled from time to time.

When we finished eating, I stood, fatigued. The day had been long. "I must leave," I said. "It's getting late."

"Let me see you to the door," Brutus said.

Nathan hugged me goodbye.

"Do well in school. Make friends."

He held me tightly. "Promise you'll come and see me."

"I will," I assured him.

Once outside, Brutus stiffened and his face tightened. "Why did you bring Nathan here?"

"He asked me to. He can be like other boys now, go to school and get married—"

Brutus cut me off. "You don't understand. Lydia doesn't know I have a son—or another wife."

I stared in disbelief.

His eyes narrowed. "It's not illegal to have two wives, you know."

I shrugged.

"In fact, it's very commonplace in her culture."

"So why don't you tell her?" I suggested. "Where is she from, anyway?"

Brutus glanced towards the door. "Egypt."

So they were speaking Egyptian. I was too weary to ask more and changed the subject. "Can you pay me the rest of what you owe—and I will be looking for other employment."

"Yeah, uh, sure. Wait here, I'll be right back." Brutus disappeared into the house.

I caught Nathan peering out the window. I looked away as if I hadn't noticed.

A few minutes later Brutus reappeared with the money. "Thank you for all your help with Nathan."

I nodded. "He's a fine son. You should be proud."

Nathan's father looked towards the ocean contemplatively. "And Shale?"

"She misses you."

"I need to get back."

I started to leave but Brutus tapped me on the shoulder. "Listen, if you wanted to stay in Caesarea for a while, until Nathan gets situated in school and adjusts, I know of a job that pays many shekels and that you'd be well suited for."

Money was the one thing I needed to pay for my medical education, and jobs that paid well in first century Palestine were limited. "What's that?"

"Gladiator."

"Gladiator?" I repeated.

"A charioteer, horse racing," Brutus clarified.

"Chariot racing?"

Anticipation was written on his face. "Yes."

I wasn't sure if he wanted me to stay in the city to spend time with Nathan or if he was sincere in wanting to help me get a good-paying job. "Tell me more."

Brutus handed me a small note. "This is the information. One of the drivers died in a race and the sponsor needs a new gladiator as soon as possible. His team has the fastest horses. You could make a lot of money—a nice living for someone as young as you."

I read his note. I had no experience with racing horses. "Why do you think I would be good at this?"

Brutus waved his hand. "The trainer can teach you everything you need to learn. The racing season just started and it lasts for several months. You win—you become wealthy."

I hesitated. "How dangerous is it?"

Brutus rubbed his eyes. "Don't fall off the chariot and you'll be fine. Besides, you're young and strong, in good physical shape."

178

A charioteer sounded exciting and the money hard to turn down. Maybe I'd delay going back to Dothan. "I'll think about it."

"Go see him now. It's not too late," Brutus said. "He will even pay your room and board. Do you have a place to stay?"

I shook my head. "No."

"It's settled," Brutus said. "Go see him, tell him I sent you, and you'll be racing soon."

I nodded. The lure of a big paycheck was tempting. If I ever made it back to 2015, I'd be set for life. I would have enough money to go to the United States and see Shale—if she made it back—and didn't marry Judd. If she married him in first century Palestine, did that mean she would marry him in 2015?

CHAPTER 33 CHARIOT RACING

As I left Brutus's villa, I again felt conflicted. I set aside my deep-seated sadness to think about chariot racing. How much money did gladiators make? Perhaps I could race for a few months, make some quick shekels, and then head back to Dothan. I would figure out how to get back to 2015. I sighed. Unexpected tears formed. Why had God abandoned me?

Shale filled my thoughts—her smile, her outbursts, her strong spirit. I stood in the street alone. The salty air stirred up memories from home. Seabirds circled overhead from the Mediterranean. While I longed to return to Dothan, I couldn't—yet. I checked my moneybag and turned south.

I tried to read Brutus's scribbled note without success. I waved to a man and spoke to him in Aramaic. "Can you give me directions?"

He stared at me. I repeated myself in Greek.

He glanced at the note and spoke too fast.

"Slow down, please. I don't speak perfect Greek."

The man complied. "You need to continue south to the theater district. You'll pass Herod's Palace. Keep going. The theater district faces the sea. If you follow the aqueduct to the Kurkar Ridge along the coast, you'll see the collecting pools and fountains as you near the theater. Follow the villa numbers. The aqueduct will exit through the tunnel and some of the ducts will go to the fountains. The residence is probably in one of those apartments by the theater."

"Thank you," I said.

"How long will it take me to get there?"

"Oh, not long. Maybe fifteen minutes."

"Thank you, again." How could I remember all of that? Talking slower didn't help.

I watched as the sun kissed the Mediterranean. The red-tinged sky reminded me of the night before the earthquake. I cleared my throat. Too much thinking made me emotional. If I didn't like what the charioteer guy said, I'd leave for Dothan in the morning.

I came to the city gates and the grandeur of the Greek and Roman buildings surprised me. How did they manage to build such opulence in the first century?

I'd studied Caesarean history, but the drawings in textbooks didn't do it justice. The aqueduct started at the foot of Mount Carmel and traveled downhill for a long distance.

I spotted where the water came out of the tunnel below the ridge. Pipes dispersed the water beautifying the city with romantic fountains. I stopped to look at one of the inscriptions. "Maintained by the second legion."

I came to Herod's Palace. The pompous mansion stood tall on a rocky high point that jutted out into the sea. Several small fountains framed the front with a swimming pool in the back.

When I passed the palace, I became aware of the roaring crowds. The hippodrome wasn't far in the distance on the city's southern shore. A wall surrounded it blocking my view. The ground shook from the pounding horse hoofs and chariot wheels.

I'd been to Caesarea a few times on school field trips. The polished white stone from the hippodrome hadn't had time to decay—it looked like marble.

I glanced at the address. I tapped another man on the shoulder. "Can you tell me where this is?"

"That way." He pointed to the villa.

I approached a two-story stone building and knocked. A stout, middle-aged man with a walking cane appeared at the door.

I greeted him. "I'm Daniel of Jerusalem, son of Aviv, a friend of Brutus, son of Dirk. He said you were looking for a charioteer."

The man sized me up, as if I were applying to be a fighter or a boxer. He didn't say anything at first.

"Did I come to the right place?" I asked.

"Come in," he said at last.

I followed the man inside. The apartment was richly furnished, similar to Brutus's although not quite as plush with the multicultural influence. Paintings of horses and chariots decorated the walls.

With nightfall approaching, oil lamps burned. I could hear a woman's voice and a child squealing in the back.

"Sit, sit," he said. "I'm Dominus. I'm the owner of the horses for the white team."

I found a chair. "It's an honor to meet you."

Dominus leaned back. "I used to race myself, until I got injured. Then I bought my own horses. Trouble is they weren't good enough. So I imported some of the finest. We pasture them when they are young on the lower slopes of Mount Argaeus. Then we bring them over to the stables when they are old enough to start training."

Dominus studied me. "How much do you know about horses?"

"I took care of Brutus's horses in Nazareth."

"I'm sure if you worked for him you must be a good worker. Know anything about driving a chariot?"

I shook my head.

"Well, I lost one of my gladiators last week—he was trampled."

I swallowed.

"I need someone to replace him. Think you can be ready in three weeks for your first race?"

"I don't know. I've never done any chariot racing."

Dominus eyed me inquisitively. "How old are you, Son?"

"Almost twenty."

"You can live in the barracks with the slaves. If I train you, you have to be indentured for a year as payback. If you win, you receive a nice paycheck for every race."

How much would that be? I was afraid to ask—yet. That might sound rude.

"But I'm the winner, not you." Dominus seemed to think this point was important.

"Do I have to live in the barracks with the slaves?"

"Do you have some money to pay room and board?"

"If you pay me, shouldn't I be able to pay for that?"

"Do you have money now?"

"Yes, from my earnings with Brutus."

"You can check around. In fact, across the street is a flat that's not too expensive."

"Can I try racing first—make sure I like it?"

"Sure. Win your first race and you get your first paycheck."

"What happens if I don't win?"

"You either win or pay off your indenture agreement by working in the mines. This sport is too expensive not to win."

Was I getting in over my head? I didn't want to look like a coward.

The man pointed his finger at me. "Can you come out tomorrow?"

I nodded.

"Great." Dominus grasped at his cane and stood, limping over to a table. He picked up an ink pen and wrote on a slip of parchment. "This is where you need to go. I'll tell Cynisca to look for you in the morning. She'll be your trainer."

"She?"

"Cynisca is the best trainer I've ever had."

I couldn't imagine being trained by a woman.

"So we are all set?" Dominus asked.

"Yes." I reached out to shake his hand. "I'll decide tomorrow and let you know for sure."

"Sounds good." Dominus walked me to the door. "Check out that boarding house. I know the owner. Tell him I sent you."

"Thank you." As I left, I waved farewell to my new employer and hurried across the street. A woman gladiator—I'd never heard of such a thing. What would that be like, to be trained by a woman? My teachers never mentioned women gladiators in history class.

A few minutes later, I entered the apartment lobby. Several Greek and Roman statues greeted me. I didn't understand why they were so ill-clothed.

An older man stood behind the counter. I gave him my name, adding that Dominus had suggested his rooming house to me.

The man smiled. "I can rent to you week-to-week. The rooms are clean."

I nodded. "Sounds good."

The man handed me a slip. "Did you just move here?"

"I'm training to be a charioteer."

He raised his eyebrow. "Dominus has the best team of horses. You will win many races. He only hires the best gladiators."

"It would be an honor to win," I replied. I paid the clerk the rent and left to find my room.

More half-naked gods and goddesses lined the hallway. I found my apartment and was pleased with its size and cleanliness. I lit the oil lamp and sat on my bed, studying the wooden walls and floor. I laid my head on the bed and soon fell asleep.

The next morning I needed to decide—should I take my money or not? I expected the training to be demanding. Did I want to risk losing it? I hid my shekels in the folds of the bed. No one had a key to the room, and I checked that the locked window was secure. I wouldn't tell anyone where I lived.

I left my apartment and snatched a quick snack from a street vender on the square. Walking past the city gates, I admired the harbor. It would rival any modern day construction in both beauty and size.

Birds circled overhead as fishermen threw their nets out for the morning catch. I'd come back later when I had more time.

I passed the hippodrome and continued south until I came to the Equi Palmati Stables. A private dirt road opened up to a large field. Five brown horses and one white horse were galloping through the pasture. The stables were barely visible from the road. To the right was a short circular dirt track.

A dark-skinned man approached me smiling.

I introduced myself. "I'm Daniel, son of Aviv, from Jerusalem, and I'm here to meet Cynisca."

The man replied, "I spoke to Dominus this morning and he told me to expect you. Come this way."

I followed him to the stables. The man opened the gate and inside the stall was a young woman. She was tall and slender, in excellent physical shape, and had her hair pulled back in a ponytail. She wore no makeup. When she saw me, she smiled.

The attendant introduced us and left. An awkward silence followed. She was wrapping a horse's leg. "Give me a second," the girl said, "and I'll be right with you."

"No problem." I stepped outside the stall and studied my surroundings. I liked being around horses again.

A few minutes later, Cynisca walked out and joined me. She interrupted my musings with her friendly chatter. "I'm glad to meet you, Daniel. May I call you Daniel?"

"Sure."

"I mean, it's all very informal here, as long as the boss isn't around."

I nodded.

"So, you want to be a gladiator?"

"A charioteer."

"You want to race?" she clarified.

"I want to try it. I told Dominus I would let him know after today."

Cynisca scrutinized me—much as I'd seen animals evaluated at a livestock show. Could I meet her standards?

She ran her fingers along my arm muscles. "Well, you're strong enough to drive a chariot. Have you ever driven one?"

I shook my head.

"I'm going to train you. Your first race is in three weeks. We'll start you with racing two horses. Once you can handle two, we'll try you with four. Four is harder to steer than two."

"All right." That sounded like a good plan.

"Let's go out front and I'll show you some things with the chariot. Tomorrow we'll continue your training at the hippodrome."

Cynisca laughed. "We'll go slowly before throwing you to the lions—just joking."

I didn't think it was funny.

She turned more serious. "You need a natural affinity, good balance, depth perception, and focus."

I could add one more quality—courage. "Sure," I replied.

Cynisca led me towards the front. She introduced me to several horses, noting which ones I seemed to prefer.

She told me about the history of chariot racing, some of her travels to Rome and Greece, where she had competed, and how they imported the horses from Africa. Every year her family made the trek, not an easy journey in first-century Palestine.

Cynisca called over the man I had met earlier and asked him to hook up two horses to one of the chariots. Once the setup was completed, she had me step up onto the chariot. When she joined me, my heart fluttered. Together we rode behind the horses on the dirt practice field. She demonstrated what to do effortlessly. I was impressed with her skill and strength.

My mind wandered. Did she have a boyfriend? How could such a beautiful young woman remain single at her age? Most women in this century were married by the time they were sixteen. She might have been twenty or twenty-one—too old for an unmarried woman.

The day passed too quickly—or maybe I was having too much fun. As evening approached, I knew I had to compete. I couldn't wait to come back the following day. I wanted to impress Cynisca. She came from a long line of gladiators. Women weren't allowed to compete in the Olympics, but they could race. She had won many races.

"So where are you staying, Daniel?" Cynisca asked, after we put the horses back in the stall.

"Close to the hippodrome, within walking distance."

"That's good," she replied. "I still live with my family. Haven't met the right one to marry yet." She tossed her head and laughed. "I'm too independent."

I respected her free spirit.

"Did your mother race?" I asked.

"Mother and Father. They named me after the famous woman gladiator from Egypt."

"It's a pretty name."

"Thank you." She stood and reached her hand out to me.

I followed her lead.

"You will be an excellent charioteer because you have the best trainer in the world."

I didn't know how to respond. She probably said that to everyone. As I strode home, I realized I hadn't thought about Shale all day. The only thing I could think about was racing—and getting to know Cynisca better.

CHAPTER 34 TRAINING

T he next day I entered the hippodrome awestruck. The pristine structure stood in ruins in my time. To see the arena in its glory now left me speechless.

I ran my hand along the kukar stone at the gated entrance. The inscription surprised me—TIBERIUM TIVS PILATUS. The Pilate stone—the only archeological evidence of the prefect's existence. I'd seen this stone in the Jerusalem museum. Would I have a chance to meet the governor?

I walked down the steps and entered through the triumphal gate. The semicircular track spread out before me. The seats extended up on all sides like a football stadium. I imagined the roar of twenty-five thousand fans, the thundering of horses, and the clamor of chariots.

A cold sweat came over me—partly from fright and partly from excitement.

Cynisca was at the flat end of the stadium by the stables. She waved. I smiled and ambled towards her. She wore what looked like a very expensive one-piece bathing suit—the female version of a charioteer's wardrobe. Her exalted status of lead trainer was obvious as others submitted to her. She didn't show a hint of intimidation from the male gladiators.

Her hair was down today, with the straight ends touching her shoulders. Her mannerisms exuded a confidence I wasn't used to seeing in a young woman, but when had I met a woman gladiator?

The men at the far end were in various stages of preparation. Most were suited up in traditional racing garb. Since I was still a trainee, I didn't have mine. Instead, I wore a rather drab brown cloak.

I was anxious to hitch up my horses. Inhaling deeply, my stomach crawled up—I should have skipped breakfast.

Cynisca greeted me. "So you decided, huh?"

"To race?"

She nodded.

"Absolutely. My mind was made up yesterday."

"I wanted to make sure. Sometimes when trainees leave they reconsider."

"I want to try it," I replied.

Cynisca placed her hands on her waist, as if going through a mental checklist. "You know it's a year-long commitment?"

That meant I'd have to stay in Caesarea longer than I wanted. If I did change my mind, though, what would they do about it? I had nothing to lose—except my life. Would not the money be worth the risk?

Before I replied, Cynisca continued. "I'm sure he'd release you after the first couple of days if you changed your mind."

"I'd doubt he'd want me racing if my heart wasn't in it."

"That would be a grave mistake," Cynisca agreed. "But the closer we get to your first race and the greater the investment in your training, the more he's relying on you."

"Is he a fair person?"

Cynisca laughed broadly. "He's never here. He shows up for the races. That's the best kind of employer, isn't it?"

She winked. "If you win, you become rich. Many have done so—if they aren't trampled by the chariots or the horses."

"Do the fans know who you are?"

"You mean do the fans know who their favorite gladiators are?"

I nodded.

Cynisca chuckled. "Sure they know. We have the most devoted followers in Caesarea. If you win, they will worship you as if you were a god. If you lose, they'll want you replaced by someone else."

I changed the subject. "Who are those men?" I pointed to the gladiators by the stables.

Cynisca followed my finger. "Oh, those are different teams. We each have a practice time on the tracks. Our slot is in about an hour with an hour allotted. You can watch a few of the teams, but I have some other things to go over with you."

"Sure."

Cynisca waved her hand. "You can learn a lot by watching others."

"I plan to do that."

Cynisca motioned. "Follow me. Let's go over some of the rules."

We walked over and sat at a shaded table. A chariot pulled by four horses passed us.

Cynisca smiled. "That's the red team. We're the white team."

"He has four horses. I thought I was racing two."

"Oh, sure, don't worry. Nidal is an experienced charioteer. He and his brother Tariq Naser are our biggest competition. I want you to study everything they do."

"I will."

Cynisca leaned over and whispered. "They're out of this world."

"What does that mean?"

Cynisca slapped her leg and laughed. "That got your attention. They were spectacular even in their first race. I have no idea where they trained. We have yet to beat them. That's why Dominus is so antsy."

"I can beat them," I said, with more certainty than I felt.

"They will try to knock you off your chariot, ram your horses."

"Is that legal?"

Cynisca scrunched up her face. "Legal? What does that mean?"

"Like rules?"

"Oh, yes, rules. Let me see what we didn't cover yesterday."

Cynisca studied her notes. "I don't think we talked about this. The chariots are modified war chariots. So when you race, you have to imagine yourself fighting—as if you were fighting to the death."

I grimaced. Sounded like an exaggeration. This was just a race. I shrugged. "Whatever."

Cynisca furrowed her brow. "You think I'm kidding, don't you?"

I shook my head. "No, but you make it sound so—so scary."

Cynisca leaned over the table. "When you're racing, you must have that killer instinct. Those gladiators are out for blood. If you don't have that killer instinct, you'll get slammed—thrown into the spina or metae."

"What's the—"

"The stone pillars. Caesar! Sounds like you've never even seen a race before."

I wasn't going to tell her I hadn't.

"Understand?"

I nodded.

Cynisca slapped the table with her hand.

I jumped.

She threw up her hands. "Show some emotion! Are you scared, excited?"

"Maybe a little of both."

She laughed. "If I can do it, you can do it. Show some passion."

"I got it."

"Good. The most dangerous points are at the turns on each side of the spina. This is where most of the collisions take place. If you lose control going into the turn, your rig can overturn, and you, along with your horses, are likely to be crushed by the other chariots as they round the post behind you."

I took a deep breath.

Cynisca probed my eyes. "Have you ever seen a man crushed by a chariot?"

I shook my head.

Cynisca sighed. "It's not a pretty sight, my friend. Even if you live, you can be maimed for life."

My stomach soured at the mere mention of crushed.

"Did you see Dominus's cane?" she asked.

192

"Yes."

"That's what happens if you get hit by another charioteer. Dominus was fortunate he wasn't killed."

"So Dominus was run over by a chariot?"

Cynisca rolled her eyes. "Not just once, many times. That's why he's a hero. A lesser man would have died, but he had the will to live."

"Have you ever wrecked?" I asked

Cynisca glanced away. "Once. After that, my father wouldn't let me race anymore. So now I'm the head trainer."

I raised my eyebrows. "And you didn't get hurt?"

Cynisca frowned. "I did, but I'm fine now. I broke some bones. I was lucky."

I hoped I was as lucky.

"The main thing is," Cynisca continued, "if you do fall off, get out of the way. Don't lie on the track like a fool."

Cynisca smacked her hands. "It can happen that fast. The best thing to do is not fall. No matter what, don't turn over your chariot. And watch out for Tariq and Nidal."

I nodded.

She glanced down at her notes. "Where was I? You were asking about rules. You can't deliberately ram into your opponent, but who's going to stop the race if someone does?"

I didn't know.

"You've got to stay clear of everyone. That's how our last gladiator was killed. He didn't and he was trampled by Nidal and Tariq."

Cynisca turned her face from me, clearing her throat before continuing.

"There are twenty-four races in a day. Most of the gladiators live in the barracks, and since you don't, you'll be a little unusual."

"In a bad way?"

"No. They'll just be curious about you. They'll think you're rich." She shrugged. "It's something you should be aware of."

"All right."

"And beware of the spikes on the sides of the chariots. Let's see, we need to get your Xystis—garment. In the meantime, you can wear the robe I gave you. Do you have a curved knife?"

"What's the knife for?"

"You don't know much about racing, do you? If you get knocked off, you don't want to be dragged by the reins of the horse. If you get tangled up, you need the knife to cut yourself loose."

My muscles tensed. Why did this have to be so dangerous?

"And, of course, we need to fit you with a leather helmet, knee pads and shin pads, and the rest of your clothing."

"When do I get those?"

"Tomorrow."

"Good."

"You'll race around the curricular seven times."

"What's that?" I interrupted.

"The arena," Cynisca clarified. "Each time you go around, they'll drop a dolphin."

"A dolphin?"

"Oh, they are in the middle. See the decorative sculptures. As you finish each lap, they tilt them forward. That's how they keep track of how many times you've gone around."

"I see."

Now, you'll be in the starting gate on the outside since you're new. Once you win a couple of races, they will give you a more preferred spot. You have to earn that."

"I will."

"And, of course, the judge's boxes will be set up the day of the race. Pontius Pilate will drop the handkerchief. And dignitaries show up, so you must do well. Otherwise, the spectators will laugh at you. They are merciless until you've proven yourself. They want a show."

Reminded me of sports back home.

"I think that's it for the rules."

"What will I wear?"

"It's a sleeveless garment called a Xystis. It comes down in a V-shape and is cinched at the waist. You'll have a pair of straps across your upper back to prevent it from ballooning up during the race. But for now, what you're wearing will work fine. We won't be racing for speed for a few days.

"Practice maneuvering the chariot through the turns, as we did yesterday, only this time in the arena. It will be more fun here, where you get a feel for the bends around the stadium."

Cynisca darted her eyes about. "It's quite exciting to be down here with all the seating and the colonnades. Don't you think?"

"Makes my stomach knot up."

She laughed. "That's good. If you didn't have some fear, I'd wonder if you were human."

I wiped the perspiration from my forehead.

Cynisca stood. "Let's head back to the stables and meet your horses."

We passed several gladiators on the way. I could feel their steely eyes, but I pretended not to notice. The Naser brothers in particular gawked at me. Of course, I wasn't dressed in the proper attire, so I looked like a newbie.

I caught up with Cynisca as we neared the entrance to the stables. The onlookers soon went back to their own business.

At least a dozen horses stood in the stalls. Each horse was tended to by two or three slaves. I was impressed with how clean the area was for so many animals.

Cynisca pointed to a chariot sitting outside a stall. "There is your bigae." The waxed front and sides made the chariot look like a piece of art. Even the wooden wheels were spotless—without a speck of dust.

Inside the stall, two slaves were grooming a horse. One of the slaves was cleaning the horse's nose—I was glad I was spared that chore—and another was shampooing the same horse's tail. Two additional slaves were tending to a second horse.

"So I'm training with these horses?"

"Yes. These are fine racehorses. Your horses," she enunciated.

I studied both of them with anticipation.

"They were specially bred in Africa."

I walked over to the closest one. His freshly brushed mane was coppery and his tail was darker, more bronze. I reached out and stroked his neck. "What are their names?"

"That one is Mosi, the lead horse. The other one is Oni."

"Greek names?"

"Of course. This is a Greek sport."

I smiled. I would soon be so fluent in Greek and Hellenistic culture I might lose my Jewishness. I had not noticed any Jews in the chariot races. I seemed to be the only one here.

Cynisca's eyes studied me as I ran my hand along the back of the horse. The slave moved out of my way.

I spoke gently to the horse. "So you are Mosi, huh? I'm Daniel and we'll make a great team, with Oni."

The horse nodded and snorted, as if understanding me.

"So even though you don't know anything about racing chariots, you seem to be comfortable with horses."

I glanced at Cynisca. "This is a fine horse, but unless he trusts me, he won't race for me."

"That's so true," Cynisca agreed. "Relationship building is important."

I stared into Mosi's eyes. If Shale were here, what secrets could she tell me about the horses?

I turned to Oni and stroked him on the neck. Both horses seemed to have good temperaments. I was glad I'd had an opportunity to meet my racing partners before we got on the track.

"Come," Cynisca said. "Let the slaves finish with the horses. They will bring the chariot and the horses out to us. Nidal and Tariq are doing their practice runs and I want you to watch."

We entered the arena and sat a few rows up in the stadium seats. The brothers were trotting around the track in their bigaes. I paid close attention to how each used his left hand to steer around the corners. Their skills impressed me. In art and athletics, whenever someone made something look easy, you knew he was skillful.

In how many races have they competed?" I asked.

Cynisca stopped to think. "They have been racing for only a few months, but they have won every race. We race every week, sometimes twice a week, so what would that be? Twenty-five races at least."

"How much money is that?"

Cynisca laughed. "They moved out of the slave quarters after their first two races. If they keep this up, they will soon become quite wealthy."

How much would medical school cost? It would take three months of working for Brutus to earn what I could win in one race—and he paid well.

I asked Cynisca, "Which is more important, the charioteer's prowess or the horse's ability?"

She puckered her mouth as she thought. "It's a little of both."

One of the brothers slapped the horse with a whip.

"I don't like slapping a horse with a whip," I commented.

"That's how you make them go faster. Horses are basically stubborn, you know."

"Not if they are trained well," I countered.

Cynisca seemed surprised by my statement. "You're in charge when you're out there racing. You must make your horse outperform the others."

I would work on the relationship part. I didn't like the whip.

After a while, the slaves brought out my bigae and horses.

Cynisca touched my hand and her bright eyes focused on me. "It's your turn now."

We walked down the steps and headed over to the chariot. My mind went blank—like right before a test at school, when I felt that I'd forgotten all the answers.

Cynisca directed me to step up on the chariot, and the slaves connected it to the horses. She handed me the reins.

"Let's go around the track slowly through the turns. Get a feel for the horses." She handed me the whip.

"You don't have to hit them hard," she cautioned. "They know what to do, but you need to let them know you're in charge."

I checked the reins. They needed to be short enough to stop the horses, but not so short that I tugged at their mouth. I would steer Mosi with my left hand and he would guide Oni on the right.

Everyone moved out of my way—probably out of fear. They knew I was a newbie.

I yelled at the horses to go. They didn't move. I tried a couple more times. They still didn't move. My face burned hot as I heard a couple of snickers from the gladiators.

Cynisca approached me. "You will have to hit them with the whip to make them go," she whispered.

I took the whip and slapped the left horse, and both horses took off running—too fast. I panicked. We came to the first turn. I blanked on what Cynisca had showed me the day before. I hoped I didn't fall off and wildly moved the reins with both hands.

As we spun out of the first turn, I breathed a sigh of relief. The horses knew what they were doing, even if I didn't know what I was doing. They made me look better than I was.

We completed the first lap around the track and I arrived back at my starting point. I noticed the slaves and gladiators looked surprised that I hadn't wrecked or fallen off the chariot.

Cynisca was all smiles. "Good job," she congratulated me, "after a somewhat dubious start."

"Can I go around again?" I asked.

"Sure. The track is ours for the next hour. Don't go too fast. Besides, you don't have your helmet. Let the horses get to know your voice today."

I galloped the horses around the track a few more times, feeling more confident each time. On the third lap, I looked up into the stands. I imagined crowds cheering as I passed victory lane.

Unexpectedly, I saw someone from my past. She sat in the first seat next to the track on the far side, wearing the same clothes I had seen her wear before. I'd almost forgotten about the ventriloquist. A year had passed since her last appearance.

She smiled and waved, holding a bag of popcorn, as if she were in the year 2015 watching a football game. Her presence was disturbing and broke my focus and concentration. What was she doing here?

I had to put her out of my mind. When I made another trip around the track, she was gone, but that she was here at all disturbed me. The demon had followed me all the way to Caesarea—why?

Cynisca walked up to me on my final lap, smiling broadly. "You did a fine job on your first day at the hippodrome."

"Thank you." My elated feeling from earlier had been subdued by the unexpected visitor. Cynisca seemed not to notice.

She peered up at the sky studying the sun's position. "It is time to finish for today. We'll be back here tomorrow first thing in the morning."

I nodded.

"You still want to be a gladiator, right?"

"Yes—absolutely."

"Good." Cynisca glanced at her parchment. "Tomorrow I'll give you your corset, helmet, shin guards, knee protectors and knife. You'll need to decide if you want to fasten the knife over your back or at your waist.

"When we take the horses up to racing speed, you'll need to wear the helmet. Accidents can happen during training."

I stepped off the chariot and stretched my muscles. I'd be sore tomorrow.

Cynisca chuckled. "You held the interest of Tariq and Nidal. They came up and asked where you're from."

"What did you tell them?"

Cynisca shrugged. "I told them I didn't know, except that you're Jewish."

I didn't say anything. An awkward silence followed.

Cynisca eyed me curiously. "Where are you from?"

"Jerusalem," I replied.

She scrunched up her nose. "Where are you staying?"

Did I want to tell her that? "Close by."

She smiled. "So you don't want to tell me, huh? I was just curious."

"I don't remember the name of the inn," I lied.

She tossed her head.

I laughed. She didn't believe me. My physical desire for Cynisca returned. I wanted to prove myself to her—that I could be the best. I knew I needed to focus on racing, though. Death or working in the mines were not good alternatives to winning. I couldn't win if I was distracted.

CHAPTER 35 THE DEMON

I left the hippodrome excited. The evening sun hung over the Mediterranean and my shadow appeared long and skinny. Now that I needed muscle mass, I was mindful of my physique.

I headed through the gates back into town. The square brimmed with activity. I grabbed some food from a street vender and walked over to an empty table. The fountain had several winged visitors playing in the spray. Stretching out on the bench, I admired the harbor.

Overlooking the harbor stood Caesar's temple. Curiosity got the best of me. What was inside that magnificent structure? Greeks frequented it throughout the day. I had never been inside a pagan temple.

After finishing my meal, I climbed the hill to see the temple up close. Was anyone watching me? Not that anyone cared, but for a Jew to enter a pagan temple would be considered scandalous by another Jew.

Why did I feel a need to be secretive anyway? I knew their gods had no power. I entered through the ornate doors and inside the hallway was a colossal statue of Caesar. I smirked that the Greeks thought Caesar was a god.

A partially clothed Roman goddess stood in a prominent location. I had no idea who she was in the hierarchy of Greek and Roman idols. The statues were beautiful as art but to believe they had supernatural powers was vexing. I didn't like being around them and left.

Once outside, I hurried across the street. I regretted my moment of frivolity. Then I saw her—the demon. No! That memory returned, when she sat cross-legged by the fire at Robbers Creek. I pretended not to see her. Somehow, I would lose her in the crowds.

Everyone seemed to be in my way. I dodged in and out of traffic, vendors, and shoppers. A ship had arrived in port and I hurried to the harbor. The influx of passengers would make me difficult to spot. I lingered in the crowds until they dispersed. Several times, I glanced around, but I didn't see her. Once I was sure she was gone, I climbed an overhanging rocky ledge. Ships filled the harbor, a hundred or more. Soon I forgot about the ventriloquist.

A wicked wind kicked up and blew sand all around below me. I was glad I was up high to avoid the particles stinging my face or getting into my eyes. I sat and watched as dark gray clouds formed. Several fishing boats pulled in their nets and headed into port. The storm grew and the tumultuous cloud formations captivated me. My better judgment told me to find cover, but I tarried.

Large droplets fell and splattered across the rocks. I climbed down and hurried back, but not before becoming drenched. I was almost to the apartment—and I saw her again. The demon was barely visible in the sheets of rain.

She walked towards me like a ghost. I ran inside the apartment lobby and raced down the hallway. Fumbling with the key, I opened the door with difficulty. After slamming it shut, I leaned against the door. Breathing heavily, I slid to the floor.

Why was she here? I knew she was evil—it was my fault. I shouldn't have entered the pagan temple.

The statue in my room had fallen over and broken into several pieces. Did I break it when I slammed the door, or did the storm shake the floor? Or had someone been in my room?

I rushed over to my bed and stuck my hand inside the blankets. My moneybag was still there. I relaxed a little. Why did I feel so jumpy?

The beheaded statue's eyes stared at me from the floor and a mocking laugh covered its face. How could something pagan like a broken statue spook me? I kicked the head across the room and it slammed into the wall. The eyes still stared back.

I stood and cracked the door. No one was around. I picked up the broken pieces and threw them in the trash.

Now I was fearful to leave. The demon saw me enter the apartment. Did she know which room was mine? I would sleep with the oil lamp burning tonight—if I slept at all.

CHAPTER 36 FIRST RACE

T hree Weeks Later

I awoke restless and sweaty. My mind swirled. Race day had arrived. I dressed and pulled the leather straps over my shoulders. The knife fit snugly in the sheath of my belt. I even took the time to fix my hair in the typical gladiator style. I would carry my helmet to the hippodrome instead of wearing it.

What would Shale think of me now? I shook off the memories to focus on racing.

The ventriloquist had not made another appearance—and my gladiator lessons had gone well—better than Cynisca anticipated. She claimed I had raised more than one eyebrow.

I closed the door and stepped outside to chattering seabirds. The sun had risen and shades of red and gold over the blue Mediterranean waters promised sunshine. The equestrian races were some of the most popular events at the venue, and the chariot races were at the top of that exclusive list.

As I walked along the streets that swelled with racing patrons, onlookers greeted me with new respect. I heard whispers, "Look, a gladiator."

Wide-eyed children delighted in my clothing. One came up and asked to touch my helmet.

The festive activities set the tone for a day of unbridled entertainment. I found a food stand and ate some pita bread with humus. I washed it down with grape juice. Then I bought a couple of trinkets from a vendor.

The celebration kicked off with a parade that began in the basilica. Each team joined in the procession, accompanied by their religious representatives, which included standards, musicians, and attending magistrates and workers.

My standard was the Dioscuri twins. One was a famed rider and the other a boxer—part of my compromise for living here. I had come to accept the hedonism. What would have disturbed me a year ago barely pricked my conscience now.

Caesarea was a Roman city and I had become like a Roman. Jerusalem was a distant memory and so was God. I had one goal—to become the most successful chariot racer who ever lived.

Outside thoughts were distractions that would keep me from winning. I was determined to beat Nidal and Tariq by any means short of cheating.

A steady breeze off the Mediterranean kept temperatures comfortable. The crowds grew as the hour of racing approached. So did my anticipation. I joined my team in the processional walk. I would only compete in the first race with two horses.

Some of the participants wore exquisite costumes that honored the Hellenistic gods. Performers, including clowns and mimes, entertained the kids. Belly dancers impressed the rest. I strained to catch a glimpse. The boundary of family entertainment was broad.

The crowds entered through a separate entrance. I spotted a family waiting in line. I waved at the young boy and he waved back. I stepped away from my team and approached them. "May I give your children a gift?" I asked the father in Greek.

The father smiled. "They would love that. Thank you."

I squatted down to eye level and handed the boy a carved wooden chariot and gladiator.

He examined the toy. "What's your name?"

"Daniel." I was surprised that the youngster spoke Aramaic.

"Thank you, Daniel," he replied.

I gave the girl, who was around nine, a carved wooden horse that matched what I gave her younger brother. She stroked the horse gently with her fingers and smiled. Then she leaned over and clasped her arm tightly around my neck. "I hope you win," she whispered.

"Thank you." I hadn't heard Aramaic since I arrived in Caesarea. The words were sweet to my ears. I went back to my spot in line, waving once more as the family disappeared from view.

As the contestants entered the hippodrome, several important magistrates greeted us. High-ranking officials sat in their decorated boxed seats. The gladiators made one trip around the track, waving to the crowds. It was another chance for the odds makers to get one last look at all the horses and charioteers.

After finishing the processional, we traipsed to the stables. We would re-enter the arena through the side entrance when the announcer shouted our names, along with each team's sponsor.

Cynisca came up to me enthusiastically. "Are you excited?"

"What?" I asked. "I can't hear you."

"Are you excited?" she repeated.

"Yes." The clamor of the crowds made it difficult to talk. I stood outside the entrance waiting, but I didn't have to wait long.

The announcer thundered my name above the roars and my knees buckled.

"Daniel, son of Aviv, gladiator from Jerusalem, making his debut appearance."

This was my moment. I bounded out and bowed promptly. I noticed that all the VIP boxes were full. Pontius Pilate sat in the imperial box, waiting to drop the handkerchief.

I waved at the crowds and the packed arena responded with cheers and applause. The whole experience was exciting— intoxicating and unforgettable. I sensed an immediate connection with the fans. Had they ever witnessed a Jew race in the hippodrome? I would do my best to whet their appetite for more.

As I returned to the stables, I caught a glimpse of the gambling tables. The counter was swarming with action. Bulging bags of shekels were exchanging hands, reminding me of the sounds made by a dinging slot machine.

I didn't know how the wagers were made, but I had added some unexpected buzz. A well-built Jewish man like me could fetch a nice prize for those who had extra wealth to play the odds.

Businessmen eyed me. They had a lot to gain—or lose. I read their minds—something I had avoided for months, but the temptation was irresistible. How good was I? Could I beat the Naser brothers?

Cynisca waved me over to the side and escorted me further away from eavesdroppers. "I heard several politicians gambling on you. Jews are respected for their work ethic and brains. Don't disappoint them."

I nodded. Then she pushed me away. "Now, go. Get to your spot. Hurry."

My two horses and chariot were already in the stall. I stepped up on the chariot and examined my surroundings. Everything appeared in order. I didn't want the race to start and find out I had been sabotaged.

I seized the reins with both hands, holding the whip in my mouth. My hands were so sweaty I wiped them on my racing garb. I switched the reins to my left hand and put the whip in my right.

This was entertainment at its best. The common folk lived week to week for the diversion it created from Roman oppression. High taxes and hard labor broke the back of the middle and lower classes. If blood was drawn or death occurred, the popularity ratings for that week's races skyrocketed.

After introducing everyone, the roar of the fans intensified. The gates would open when Pontius Pilate dropped the handkerchief. I was in the outside lane.

The raucous crowds clamored for the races to begin. The trumpet sounded. Pontius Pilate stood in the box holding the handkerchief. My moment had come.

I started to wrap the reins around my waist, as was the custom in Roman racing. That allowed the gladiator to hold the whip with his hand, but since I didn't need to slap my horses with the whip except once at the start, I changed my mind. Why not just hold the reins instead? I could clench the whip with my teeth.

Leaning forward I braced for the gate to open. Despite the cool breeze blowing off the Mediterranean, sweat beaded up on my face and neck. The crowds stood, all eyes fixed on Pontius Pilate.

The trumpet blew and the prefect dropped the handkerchief. The horses lunged out of the starting gates. I slapped the whip on Mosi's rump and we were off. The horses' powerful hindquarters rose and fell as I held the reins and let them gallop. I wouldn't need to slap the horses again.

My job was to keep them away from danger, which lurked even before the first turn. With so many chariots on the first lap, the greatest worry was bumping into another racer.

The lead horse set the pace. I maneuvered my chariot around those chariots closest to me, even though it cost me valuable time

The horses came out of the first turn and the stadium vibrated. Dust filled the track making it difficult to see.

Suddenly the rider on the chariot in front of me fell. I snapped the reins to the left and swerved. Could the chariots behind me avoid running over him? Officials dispatched the medics to retrieve the fallen gladiator. The unmanned chariot overturned. I passed it as the hapless horses kept going. I forged ahead.

The crowds stomped and screamed. The excitement escalated. Blood spilt made the fans thirsty for more.

Before the second dangerous turn, I pulled up alongside three others. Two of the racers were nearer the spina and galloped ahead. One tried to force the other into the center. The columns and statues created deadly obstacles.

The team to my right edged perilously close. I cracked the whip. The horses responded. Clenching the whip between my teeth, I held the reins with both hands. I used every ounce of strength I possessed to guide the horses away from the reckless charioteer who wanted to bump me.

The other chariots to my left lurched forward. The leader was still undetermined. I rushed to fill the gap.

We careened around the third turn. The charioteer to my right pressed in on me. The horses felt it and sped up. My heart thumped louder.

We were on the far side of the track when two chariots slammed into each other. One of the gladiators had slashed his competitor with the whip. The second one retaliated. The chariots sped down the raceway out of control and overturned. I galloped over bloodied arms and legs. Horses' cries and the screech of splitting metal filled the stadium.

Soon the first dolphin fell. Six chariots remained with six more laps to go.

Two chariots passed me. I couldn't tell where I was. If three were in front, that meant two were behind me.

The second dolphin fell. Five more laps to go. I heard another chariot crash—must have been behind me. I didn't see anything straight ahead.

I soon passed the wreckage of two overturned chariots. The medics had already carted off the bodies. Did that mean three other chariots were still in the race? I couldn't be sure.

Another dolphin dropped, four more laps to go. Dust and carnage covered large portions of the track. Medics ran out to retrieve the injured or dead, time permitting. Maybe I could win by attrition.

I urged my horses to go faster but avoided the use of the whip. They obeyed. My confidence grew. I approached another chariot. The gladiator charged into my path, resisting my encroachment. The determination to win had now turned to viciousness. I would wait. We rounded the curve. I was too close. If he wrecked, I would hit him. I backed off. I tried to ease to the middle. The charioteers closed the narrowing gap. Tariq and Nidal ferociously held their positions. The hysteria reminded me of a soccer game. I saw my opportunity to take the lead dwindling. I was so close with only three other charioteers in the race.

Another dolphin fell. Three more laps to go.

One of the Naser brothers exited the track by the stables. Something must have happened.

The dust had settled with fewer horses. I must avoid the carnage to finish. I stayed as close to the spina as I dared. Two charioteers were still in the race.

Two more laps to go.

I urged my horses to charge. They responded. I passed another chariot. I was second gaining on the leader.

Another dolphin fell. One more lap to go.

The roaring crowds wanted a climactic finish. My horses tasted victory—and they were hungry. I slapped my reins but didn't strike the animals with the whip. They seemed to whip themselves.

We rounded the final bend. I was side by side with the only charioteer left. His eyes met mine. He whipped his horses. I urged mine to surge ahead.

We gained. The out-of-control crowd stood and cheered as the finish line approached. In a last-second display of determined strength, we edged out the leader.

The dolphin fell. We'd won!

The crowd went crazy. I waved at the cheering fans and looked for Cynisca but didn't see her. A mob had congregated around the judges' tables. The betting arena was thick with patrons. No one seemed happy.

Why wasn't anyone congratulating me? The slaves who took care of the horses approached.

"Didn't I win?" I asked.

"Your win is being contested by the Naser brothers."

"Why?"

"They say you cheated."

Anger welled up. I bolted over to the judge's area, dodging fans and others in my way. An angry protest had grown and harsh voices shouted over one another.

I saw Cynisca. She was talking to an official. I ran up to her.

The VIP said, "We need to let the judges decide if he meant to cheat. Since it's his first race, they may let him off with just a fine, calling it a foul. You need to make sure your team knows the rules."

"Caesar! My team knows the rules."

The man crossed his arms. "You may but your gladiator doesn't."

"What's the matter?" I asked. "What did I do wrong? I won—didn't I?"

Cynisca glared at me. "One of the Naser brothers claims you cheated and has asked that your win be stripped."

I stared at Cynisca. "What did I do?"

"Why did you not wrap the reins around your waist as you did in practice?"

That was the infraction? "Attaching the reins to the waist makes it easier to slap the horses with the whip. I don't have to do that."

"But it's the tradition in Roman racing to tie them around your waist."

"What difference does it make?"

Cynisca shrugged. "It shouldn't make any, but I sure wished you'd done it the way you were trained. Why would you change things on your first race without asking?"

I shook my head. "I didn't think it was a big deal. I just decided to hold the reins. Maybe I was nervous, I don't know."

Dominus approached us with great difficulty in the crowds. It was the first time I had seen him today. He looked angrier than a savage shark. He yelled at Cynisca, "Why didn't you train Daniel properly?"

"I did," Cynisca protested. "He changed it on his own."

His bulging eyes blasted fiery torpedoes at me. I didn't want to look at him. "I'm sorry."

"You ask before you do anything different from how you've been trained, boy. Understand?"

"Yes."

"I'm facing a fine now, and they could disqualify you from further racing."

I hung my head, unable to think. Cynisca walked off leaving me alone. I felt dejected and humiliated. I went and sat in a corner to wait for the official's ruling.

The crowd had become antsy. They wanted a winner announced. I threw my helmet down on the ground and watched it roll away. What a wasted effort, all because I held the reins rather than attaching them to my waist.

The stadium noise shot up another notch. A winner had been shouted over the commotion. I hurried over to see the decision. Cynisca shook her head.

Who won? I walked up to the judges' table and saw the official result. Tariq Naser, followed by several names I didn't recognize—all of whom had either died or been knocked out of the race. They didn't even record my name.

The crowd had gone wild, throwing food and personal items over the seats of other patrons. Roman soldiers had gone up into the stands to bring order. Fighting had spread among the fans and the chaos swelled.

I glanced at Pontius Pilate who stood watching. Many in the stands were chanting my name. Most fans were unhappy that Tariq stood in the spina to receive the laurel crown and not me.

Could I do anything to quiet them? This was my fault and if anyone got hurt, I would feel responsible.

Much to my relief, after several minutes, the Roman soldiers brought order, removing those who were inciting the others.

Preparations were under way for the second race. The delay had given the attendants more time to clear the debris from the track.

I walked over and sat by the entrance—wishing I could do it over again. I tried to look at the positive side. I wasn't dead like the gladiators carted off. I'd live to race anther day.

A few minutes later, the young girl to whom I had given the toy horse walked towards me. I was surprised she found me, but I suppose in my racing outfit, I wasn't that hard to spot. She handed me a box.

"What is this?" I asked her.

"Open it," she said. I glanced behind her, and her father and brother were watching us a short distance away. I couldn't imagine what was in the box. I opened it and pulled out a laurel crown.

"Where did you get this?"

"God told me to give it to you," she said in Aramaic.

I turned the crown over and examined it. It looked identical to the one won by the winners.

"It's beautiful. Thank you."

"It's yours," the girl said.

I grinned. "I need all the luck I can get. Thank you."

She nodded and ran back to her father and brother. I waved at them and mouthed, "Thank you." They waved back and headed to their seats.

What a special gift that I didn't deserve.

CHAPTER 37 REVENGE

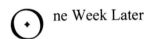ne Week Later

Gossip about the way the officials had stripped my win made the headlines throughout Caesarea. Many thought it was unfair. Others sided with the Naser brothers. No doubt, the debacle created more interest in the races for the following week and a sympathy factor for my team. Everyone wanted to know about the Jewish gladiator who had instigated the controversy.

When Dominus realized many fans believed I was disqualified unfairly, he eased up on the verbal thrashings.

Cynisca had taken to repeating instructions, which created tension between us. She no longer trusted me. I'd have to earn that back. Still, I was excited to race again.

Something else was different. The Naser brothers didn't let me out of their sight in the hippodrome. They knew I could beat them.

I had won the hearts of many even though Tariq had been declared the official winner. To lose the sympathy vote of the fans on a technicality had been at great cost, probably more than the brothers had anticipated. The accusation of cheating had deepened the loyalty factor for those who supported me. I had fans who wanted me to win as payback.

I surmised the reason the older brother had left the race was to tell the officials of my infraction, ensuring the younger brother would be declared the winner by default.

I had to let it go and move on. I sat in the stall talking to the horses, Mosi and Oni, as the slaves prepped them for the race. Today both horses would have their mane braded with pearls.

I stroked Mosi's neck. "You run like you did last week and we will win. You are the fastest horse—except for Oni." I smiled. "And the strongest."

The slave nodded as he brushed the horse's mane. "You will win today. I know it."

I chuckled. "Thanks for believing in me."

Everything happened as before, with the introductions and formalities. The hippodrome was packed even more than the previous week. I would be racing fifth.

My race time came and the crowd responded with loud cheers when the announcer shouted my name above the roars. Fans clapped. Surprised by the show of support, I didn't want to disappoint them.

The middle gate was a better position from which to start. I made sure to attach the reins around my waist. I checked repeatedly that the knife was secure in the sheath if I needed it.

Once again, Pontius Pilate was the official handkerchief dropper. At the sound of the trumpet, he dropped the mappa. The gates opened and we were off.

I held the whip in my hand but never touched the horses. They ran like the wind. I sensed the horses of the past in them, the great ones that pulled the chariots of the one true God.

Maybe the horses' bloodlines even went back to the horses of Elijah and Elisha. The animals ran as heavenly spirits. Their passion, power, and splendor radiated in every step they took. I looked out into the stands. Cheers and applause swept away any doubt about who was the fastest.

The first dolphin fell. There were no horses or chariots to dodge, though I heard the splintering of wood and clashing of metal behind me. The medics descended on the track to clear the carnage. Where were the Naser brothers? I remembered the story of Sodom and Gomorrah. I shouldn't look back.

Each lap around the track, a dolphin fell, bringing me closer to victory. Anticipation rose—and so did my heart rate. I wanted this more than I had ever wanted anything. I coaxed Mosi and Oni to keep going, not to let up, that the race was ours to win.

We rounded the final bend on the final lap and approached the finish line. I looked straight ahead. As we approached, the heavens opened. Rushing wind swooped down on the hippodrome and lifted the chariot. It seemed as if we were racing on air effortlessly. Peels of thunder reverberated overhead and blazing rays of light poured out of the sky. Was I driving a chariot of God? We crossed the finish line to the deafening crescendo of roaring crowds that shook the stadium. I raised my hands triumphantly.

The remaining chariots soon rolled gloomily over the finish line. I stepped off my chariot and hugged Mosi and Oni. They were exceptional horses. How many shekels had I won?

Cynisca ran up to me and gave me a hug. "Congratulations on your first win." Tears streamed down her face.

I leaned into her. "Thank you."

Dominus joined the rest of us and the whole stadium erupted when I stood in the spina to receive my crown. I waved to the fans. I was a star—the center of attention. I felt a strange surge of power pass through me. Is this how powerful people felt, movie stars and politicians and sports icons? I knew God had allowed me to win, but I didn't feel close to him. I didn't know why, although I didn't care either.

When I walked out of the arena, the older Naser brother, Nidal, walked up to me. He reached out his hand. "Congratulations."

I breathed a sigh of relief. I had feared something else. When I looked at his arm, I saw a tattoo. Did people have tattoos in first century Palestine? Nidal's hand was extended. I clasped it. "Thank you."

Then he walked away. If I had access to the Internet I'd do a Google search. I had seen that image before, but I didn't know where.

CHAPTER 38 RECKONING

Seven Weeks Later

I won every race I entered. Cynisca encouraged me to begin training with four horses.

"You'll make more money if you win," she said.

I had grown attached to Mosi and Oni. I hated thinking about the emotional energy required to bond with two more horses. Besides, even racing with just two, my money had grown faster than I could have imagined.

"People want to see you race with four," she insisted. "They have never seen anyone race like you."

"What do you mean?"

Cynsica thought for a moment. "Magic takes over when you step on the chariot. The fans see it. They want more."

I couldn't deny it. I loved the spotlight. Being recognized by strangers on the streets was sweet. I had become a hero to many kids. More than that, I loved racing with Mosi and Oni. I didn't think I would have as much success with four horses. The dangers of getting injured or killed quadrupled.

"Give me another month," I said. "You already have great teams in place racing four. I would upset them if they thought I wanted their position."

"But they aren't winning, Daniel," Cyncisa insisted. "And Dominus is antsy. He wants you to take one of those spots."

219

"Tell him I will in a month."

Cynisca sighed. "Come close," she said.

We had lots of extra time since my race was later in the day. I walked over and sat beside her on the bench. She stood behind me and rubbed my back and shoulders.

My muscles had ached for weeks. "I didn't know you knew how to give back massages."

Cynsica laughed. "I didn't think you would let me."

I wanted to melt under her expert fingers. "So why now?"

"You seem tense. I know your muscles must be sore. I was once a gladiator, too, you know."

I couldn't argue with her.

"There are places in Caesarea you can go for a full rubdown," she remarked.

I had seen those rooms, but I didn't think a Jewish man would be welcomed. More than body massages took place behind those pagan walls. Despite my wanderings, I was still pure and intended to remain so until I married.

As I reflected on recent conversations with Cynisca, I sensed she wanted more in our relationship. My thoughts always returned to Shale. I liked Cynisca, though. If only I knew whether Shale had married Judd. Maybe she had returned to her time. Cynisca had a charm all her own that infatuated me. A woman who had such wits in a man's world earned my admiration.

My thoughts turned to more practical matters. How much money had I won? I didn't know how to equate it to American dollars in 2015, but I hoped my college tuition would be covered. Would a hundred thousand dollars pay for the cost of a U.S. school like Stanford? Of course, if I went to a state school it would be much less.

Was there a medical school near Atlanta? I loved being rich.

I left the hippodrome to get a bite to eat, feeling more confident than ever. Passersby waved at me.

"Look, Daniel, the charioteer," a young lad said to his mom in Greek.

"Yes, you are quite right. It is." They waved and I waved back. I had not seen the Jewish family since that first night.

The races started as usual early in the morning, but my race was later. I found it draining to sit all day inside the hippodrome, so I made a couple of visits to the food court. After eating, I headed back.

The roar of the crowds cheering on their favorite racer was deafening. The slaves were still prepping my horses.

I spoke kindly to Mosi and Oni and gave them each a sweet treat. Perhaps more out of superstition than anything else, the slaves pearled the mane of the horses in the same way as when I had won my first race.

"How are you doing?" I asked the slaves. They worked hard and rarely received the recognition they deserved.

"We are doing fine," the young Egyptian said. He was about my age. "We are praying you have a good race today."

"Thank you." Who was their god? I was afraid to ask.

Soon the announcer called my race. I went to the starting gate where I held the pole position. Sometimes the crowds thinned as the day wore on, but today the stadium overflowed with patrons, some forced to stand and watch from the aisles.

Many had stayed only to see me. My fame had spread beyond Caesarea—as the Jew who raced with horses and a chariot of the one true God.

People chanted my name and the fans even invented their own form of a human wave machine. They would start at one end and travel to the other. The visual effect was stunning.

When the flowers that had been thrown on the track were removed, all eyes turned to Pontius Pilate. He dropped the handkerchief and the gates flew open. The track became a sea of horses and chariots.

Mosi and Oni nosed out the other horses as they galloped across the stadium. I had not laid the whip on them in weeks. The race went by briskly with the usual casualties, the usual carnage, the usual dolphins, the usual crown. The races were no longer exciting to me.

I had grown accustomed to the usual ho-hum and pretended it didn't bother me, even though it did. I had to compromise on some things, but I wasn't proud of it.

On this day, despite my win, I didn't feel the usual high. Perhaps I was tired. I stood and waved at the fans from the spina. They had come to see a good show and I had delivered. When I turned to leave, I heard a familiar voice, but I couldn't place it. The words were in Aramaic.

"Daniel, it's Simon."

I searched for the man in the twilight. No, it couldn't be. The only Simon I knew was a leper from years ago. I vaguely remembered Dr. Luke telling me the rabbi had healed him.

The man approached waving his arms and smiling. He thrust his hand out for me to shake it. I stared into his eyes with disbelief.

"Don't you remember me?" he asked. "I'm Simon, the leper."

I shook my head. "No. I mean yes."

We laughed and hugged each other. I stepped backed to examine him. I saw no lesions on his face or his body.

"I'm healed," said Simon.

"How?"

"You'll never believe it, but Yeshua, the rabbi from Nazareth, healed me."

I hadn't heard that name since I had arrived in Caesarea. My mind reflected back to meeting the rabbi—and Nathan's healing. I was caught off-guard and didn't know what to say.

Simon leaned over and looked into my face in the approaching darkness. "You do know who that is?" he asked.

"Yes, I do. We just don't hear much about rabbis in Caesarea and I'd forgotten about him."

Simon shook his head. "I don't like what this place is doing to you, Daniel. You are becoming one of them."

"What do you mean by one of them?"

"A pagan," Simon said.

Anger welled up. What right did he have to judge me? I remained silent and started walking.

"Come on, Daniel. You know this isn't right for you. You are a Jew and living a lie."

I stopped and faced him. "If you came all the way here to tell me that, you're wasting your time." Then I started walking again, kicking a rock with my sandal in frustration. It skidded across the ground and hit a statue in the heart. "What are you doing here in Caesarea anyway?"

Simon seized me from behind and stood close, invading my personal space. I backed away.

"Are you afraid of me or something? I don't have leprosy anymore."

"No."

Most of the people had left the hippodrome and slaves were cleaning up the trash. I saw a table and motioned for him to join me. We could talk undisturbed. The thirty seconds walking over gave me time to cool down. What right did he have to judge me for earning a respectable living?

I plopped down on the bench and changed the subject. "How is your family?"

He scooted in front of me on the other side. "Much has happened since I last saw you."

I reached back in my thoughts to those first days after I arrived in Dothan. How innocent and young I was. "It's been over three years, hasn't it?"

Simon nodded. He cleared his throat. "Yeshua is the Messiah."

"Oh!" I replied.

"He is."

"You came all the way here to tell me that?"

Simon leaned forward undeterred. "Daniel, God sent me to tell you. You've become quite famous in the last couple of months. Once I realized the Daniel people were talking about was you, the Jewish charioteer, I had to come see you. My, but you've changed."

What was that supposed to mean. "How?"

Simon shrugged. "Will you be attending the Passover?"

"You didn't answer my question. How have I changed?"

"When is the last time you cared about someone besides yourself? Are you ever going to earn enough money? You've become self-serving, consumed by worldly passions, reveling in the pagan idol worship that God forbids."

"That's enough." I glared at the man. I stood and paced, seething with anger. "I'm making a living, saving money for college. What's wrong with that?"

"Come back with me," said Simon. "You need to meet the Messiah. He will set you free—from all of this." Simon waved his hand—in a stadium filled with pagan gods and goddesses.

"No," I said flatly.

"Will you at least come to Jerusalem for Passover? When is the last time you offered a sacrifice?"

I didn't respond.

Simon stood to leave. "God sent me to you and I have done as he asked. I go in peace, my friend." He reached out to shake my hand.

I reluctantly shook it but refused to look him in the eyes. I didn't want to admit he was right. I had grown comfortable in my lifestyle and wanted to keep racing.

"I'd love to serve you dinner in Bethany if you come for Passover next month. Ask anybody around the area. They can direct you to my house."

"Thank you," was all I could say.

Simon left, leaving me standing alone. A dolphin fell. The sky had darkened, as had my heart. What had I become?

CHAPTER 39 THE DREAM

A misty wind cut through me as I trudged back home. A heavy fog made it difficult to see. The cold raindrops felt like ice pellets and the waves pounding the rocky cliffs of the Mediterranean portended an approaching storm.

The strange weather reflected my distorted reality. Why was I here? Uneasiness swept over me. What did God want from me? How could I have strayed so far from my faith? I wasn't even sure if I believed in God anymore, but he had brought me here. I pointed my finger at the heavens. "You hear that, God? You brought me here."

I couldn't see through the misty fog, but something or someone was nearby. I heard heavy breathing and mocking laughter.

A door slammed and a foul odor turned my stomach. The darkened sky opened and heavy raindrops mercilessly bore down on me. I sloshed through the storm as occasional lightning pierced the darkness.

The temporary light revealed the building straight ahead. The darkness that followed, though, was even blacker.

I counted my steps—one, two three, four, five—and strained forward as thunder shook the ground. I came to the portico and stumbled at the rise. The attendant had already locked the entrance. I pounded on the wooden door.

Someone opened it. I fell through the entryway and collapsed on a chair, dripping. When I looked up to see who had let me in, the room was empty.

The door creaked back and forth and a gush of wind-driven rain pelted me in the face. I ran over and shut the door.

I looked around. Did I lock someone out? I couldn't leave some poor soul outside in this miserable weather. Who let me in?

Another lightning bolt lit up the room followed by violent thunder. The room rattled. Guilt got the best of me. I unlocked and cracked the door. "Anyone there?"

Falling rain was the only noise besides my labored breathing. Could it have been my imagination? Maybe the wind blew the door open. I called once more. "Anyone out there?"

Lightning revealed no one lurking in the shadows. I slammed the door shut and locked it. When I turned around, the room was still empty. I ran back to my apartment. Once inside, I checked three times to make sure I locked the door. My eyes scanned the room. I ran over to the bed. Underneath the blankets, my shekels remained hidden. Nothing seemed missing. I tried to inhale and exhale normally but my emotions betrayed me.

After stripping off my wet clothes and putting on something warm, I climbed underneath the covers, but I couldn't quit shaking. The room was too dark. I reached over and lit the oil lamp. I would sleep with the light on tonight. I scooted back underneath the covers and stared at the ceiling. Soon I drifted off, but dreams that seemed too lifelike to be imaginary and too dreamlike to be real disturbed any restful sleep that might have come.

I saw a stone castle at the edge of a steep precipice. The citadel guarded a country unfamiliar to me. A golden swath of light emanated from within the old fortress, or maybe it came from behind the structure—or both. The light drew me towards what was an ancient castle.

Two towers flanked the gloomy building on each side. The ray of luminosity stopped abruptly at the front of the fortress forming a round floating sphere. It looked like a large transparent bubble, but I couldn't see through it.

A narrow road scaled the rocky precipice. I kept fighting the sensation of falling as I climbed. The castle reminded me of the

Tower of Babel—high above everything else. Wispy clouds surrounded it and gave it a floating appearance.

I shivered as an icy breeze cut through me. Climbing the slippery surface, I wished I had cleats on the soles of my shoes. I relished every breath as I gulped in the thin air.

Once I made it to the top, I turned around to see how high I was. The country below seemed small and insignificant. The castle beckoned me.

I walked through the door and flaming torches lined the hallway. Several doors to adjoining rooms flanked each side of the entryway.

The foyer led to stairs at the back of the castle that wound in a corkscrew to the second floor. I tried to open the first door in the foyer but it was locked. I tried another and another, but to no avail.

I gave up on the doors and crept towards the back.

The sound of my footsteps on the marble floor echoed through the empty room. I was afraid someone might hear me, but the castle seemed vacant—forgotten in time.

I was searching for something, but I didn't know what. The stairs creaked as I stepped on each one. I reached the top and stood before a large door. Upon opening it, a darkened rectangular room spread out in front of me. In the shadows at the far end, a man was chained to the wall, but I couldn't see his face.

I heard voices and footsteps coming up the stairs behind me. I froze. My legs wouldn't move. I pulled on one of my legs with my hands to lift my foot, but my leg was too heavy. I fell to my knees and scooted myself across the floor, hiding behind a chest of drawers. Two men entered, but I didn't recognize them. They walked past me, speaking in Arabic. I tried to understand their words, but I couldn't.

I watched from behind the chest. The two men approached the prisoner. One of them spoke to him, but I didn't understand the Arabic.

I heard the voice of the prisoner. He spoke in Hebrew, "I'm not going to tell you where it is."

I heard my father's voice.

I woke up hyperventilating. Could my father be alive holed up in a castle somewhere? Who were those men? After a few moments, I came to my senses.

It was a dream—only a dream. I wanted something familiar to cling to, a tether to keep from falling—as if I could still fall off the mountain.

I sat on my bed and sobbed. I missed my father. I missed my home—my country, my time, my friends. I didn't know how to get back. Even if I could, I wouldn't. I had agreed to race for the next eight months.

Honor meant I kept my word. I reached for my shekels under the covers—my gold, my golden idol. I would finish my time here and go back to Dothan and ask God to help me—just a little more money, a few more races.

I was no General Goren—and no angel either.

CHAPTER 40 FINAL RACE

T wo Weeks Later

The crowds stood and cheered when I walked into the stadium. I was the gladiator everyone had come to see. The sponsors wanted to maximize the profits and build the suspense—so my race was last. I had become a hero in Caesarea and beyond.

I waved to my fans. What else did they have to look forward to besides chariot racing? I gave the masses a diversion from cursed Rome.

I admired the stadium, its construction, its history, and the lore of chariot racing. The excitement it offered to those in the stands and the courage of those who dared to step onto a chariot and be a gladiator—I was part of that story now that been forgotten, but had I let it go too far?

I wrapped the reins around my waist and tucked the knife inside the sheath. The slaves loaded the horses into the starting gates. The trumpet sounded, the handkerchief dropped, and the gates flew open.

Was this just a game, a race, or more? In the beginning, I wanted shekels to pay for my medical education. What did God want?

As the horses ran with the strength of a mighty wind, I looked up into the darkened sky. Suddenly another dimension peeled back. Heaven and earth revealed themselves as a scroll that opened. The words on the scroll took on life itself—scenes played out in the heavens. The dimension of earth and the dimension of heaven had collided into a transcendent world visible only to my spiritual eyes.

I suddenly became aware of the battle between good and evil, a battle of gigantic proportions. I was surrounded by spiritual beings both beautiful and terrifying.

Demons and angels sat alongside racing patrons in the stands—as well as other strange creatures for which I had no name. The old familiar smell of rotten eggs filled my nostrils and burned my throat. Where was the ventriloquist? My stomach had soured and I feared I would throw up.

My knees buckled and I swayed out of control. I was racing in a race of a different kind. I didn't know I had entered this race. I gradually perceived this was a race for my soul. Someone else had taken over the reins.

Creatures filled the skies, heavenly creatures wielding clanging swords and deadly weapons. The skies revealed a real heaven and a real hell locked in a spiritual battle of immense proportions.

I wanted to steer my chariot towards the heavens, where goodness was gaining strength as it fought back against the darkness, but I was no longer in control of my life. Had it been ripped from me or had I given it up unawares? Why had I made so many poor choices?

The masses roared with profane words and hearts captivated by worldly pursuits and unholy passion. Their shouts exploded across heaven and earth. I became keenly aware that every word we uttered was heard in other dimensions and not just in time and space. Could the spiritual world be more real than physical reality?

Mosi and Oni galloped down the course as a storm-wind descended in the form of a spirit. The breeze blew around the chariot, like a heavenly messenger delivering a special gift. I came to realize I was not just a racer, but the prize itself. Something or someone wanted me—badly.

The horses morphed into fiery beastly cherubs pulling the chariot. Two more angels appeared on either side. The four powerful winged creatures surrounding the chariot again morphed into indescribable shapes, terrifying creatures that hurtled the chariot across the track and into the heavens. I had no concept of where I was. Heaven and earth had melded as one.

Above the frightening horses of fire was a glass ceiling. On the ceiling was a magnificent throne. Seated on the throne was someone who had the appearance of a man and the likeness of God. His radiance blinded me and my knees buckled. I started to fall off the chariot, but a hand reached out and caught me. Fire blazed all around—I was riding in a chariot of fire like Elijah rode into heaven—the Merkabah.

The man's legs glowed like molten lava. He wore a crown—but I couldn't read what was written on it. The mysterious man's face shone like the sun. Pure white light bathed his garments. He had the appearance of the glory of God. I wanted to fall down and worship him, but he told me to stand.

I looked up and saw the heavens. Above the stadium, scenes scrolled across the sky. I saw the creation of heaven and earth, the Garden of Eden, and the fall. I saw Abraham bind Isaac as an offering to God and the willingness of each to be obedient unto death.

I saw the anguish of Joseph, rejected and betrayed by his own brothers—a young man who suffered unfairly from false accusations and slander, though he himself was righteous. I felt Joseph's pain when his brothers did not recognize him.

What was the significance? Why did Joseph not reveal his identity to his brothers until their second trip to Egypt?

"It was a test," the man on the throne said.

Two goats appeared. One goat was sacrificed. "Atonement must be made," the mysterious man said. The other one was driven into the desert. The man said, "I am doing a new thing."

"What new thing?" I asked.

The man read my thoughts. "Everything must be fulfilled that is written in the Law of Moses, the Prophets, and the Psalms."

Where was this written? Who was the heavenly being in the Merkabah? As I looked around, the chariot appeared to resemble the ark—God had opened my eyes to understanding things far above my natural ability.

Two Jews removed a man from a tree. I caught their faces, the faces of enlightened Jews who loved more than the rest. They loved the one on the cross the most.

Fires around Jerusalem filled the sky and the temple burned. The city mourned.

Swift-moving scenes revealed more suffering and sorrow— centuries came and went.

Fire reached up into the heavens. The whole sky blazed with the fires of Auschwitz. I watched as my mother's grandmother and grandfather walked to their deaths in the gas chambers.

"No, no," I cried.

Two prominent Jewish men secretly took the crucified man down from the cross and buried him in a rich's man tomb. Later the tomb was empty.

Scenes came and went, faster and faster. The vision ended with General Goren fighting on the plains of Megiddo. Someone found him and transported him to the hospital in the Old City. He lay near death. I saw an angel visit him, but I couldn't see his face.

The mysterious man spoke. "Today you were to die in an accident, but your life is spared because your work is not yet finished. You have been marked—sealed as a servant of God. Remain pure and undefiled. Beware of the evil one who wants to profane you and take away your crown."

Suddenly the chariot spun out of control. I fell and felt my body being stretched too far. Pain surged through my joints and ligaments. A bright light surrounded me. Two creatures lifted me and carried me over to the spina. Then they laid me down in the grass.

I felt someone hovering over me, but my vision was blurry and I couldn't see. The medics came, placed me on a cot, and carried me somewhere.

I heard Cynisca asking the medic, "Is he still alive?"

"Yes. He is very fortunate," a voice replied.

I tried to speak, but I couldn't. I could move my arms and legs and feel my limbs, but my mind was reeling.

After a few minutes, my vision returned. I touched my eyes— my contacts were gone. How could I now see without my contacts? The medic applied a cool cloth to my face and wiped off the blood.

Cynisca stood beside me. She leaned over and smiled. "Thank Caesar you're all right."

"And the horses?" I asked.

"The chariot became separated from the horses and the animals kept going. The horses behind you didn't fare as well. You flew through the air and landed in the grass. It's amazing you weren't killed."

I nodded.

The medic bandaged up the cuts on my arms and legs. I remembered vaguely what had happened. The races were over for the day and people were leaving. Several stopped by to check on me. I tried to stand, but I was too dizzy.

Cynisca frowned. "Daniel, why don't you let me take you back to my place and you can rest. I can fix you some food and change your bandages."

"Sure," I said. "If you can."

"I'll be back in a few minutes."

She left for a short time, which gave me a few minutes to recuperate. I felt extremely fatigued and wanted to sleep. When she returned, concern covered her face. She spoke gently. "Do you feel well enough to walk? I have just the spot for you to recover."

I grimaced. "I don't know."

"Here," she said. "Let me help you."

She squatted down beside me and I draped my arm over her shoulder.

"Just walk slowly," she encouraged me. "No need to rush."

Once I stood on my feet, some strength returned. Leaning on her as I limped along, she took me to a beautiful apartment on the water, not far from my own apartment. Fortunately, it was very close to the hippodrome.

The picturesque dwelling overlooked the Mediterranean. We walked around to the back of the apartment instead of going inside. Did she have a key or did she just want to see the sunset? Red streaks filled the horizon.

"Is this your place?" I asked.

"No. I asked the owners if we could borrow it for tonight."

"I remember you said you lived with your family."

"Yeah. Well, I started thinking you may not want to go to a Gentile's house so I brought you here instead. The view is beautiful and the place restful."

"So whose apartment is this?"

"A friend. It's no big deal. They won't mind if we hang out here for a few hours."

I leaned on the rail overlooking the sea. Hungry sea gulls darted about in the rocky dunes looking for whatever sea gulls ate.

"Do you mind if I lie down?" I asked.

"Sure. You can lie down on this low table and I'll massage your shoulders."

I stretched out and dozed while Cynisca went inside. She soon returned carrying a drink, large towel, and tray with heated stones. She set the tray on the table, along with the towel. The aroma from the stones reminded me of Martha's mint tea.

Cynisca lit the torches on the portico as darkness fell. The lights flickered and I let my mind wander.

She walked over and sat beside me. "How are you feeling?"

"Better." I reached out and touched her arm.

Cynisca appeared uncharacteristically edgy. Maybe she felt uncomfortable away from the stables and the racetrack. She studied my face as she clasped the drink with both hands. She smiled and rubbed her hand along my forehead. "What is that mark?" she asked.

I reached up and touched it. "A scar from a long time ago. I don't remember how I received it."

She smiled. "It looks like a seal."

"What do you mean? It's just a scar."

"Like what the Roman use for important documents."

I had recently heard that word, but I couldn't remember where.

"If you turn over, I can start on your back first."

I turned over on my stomach and Cynisca covered me with the towel. She applied the lotion and her expert hands rubbed the oil deep into my pores. The hot stones on my sore shoulder muscles felt heavenly.

My mind retraced the race as if it were a dream. Who was the mysterious person in the chariot? What happened? My life had been spared—but why? Then I remembered the words, "You have been sealed—remain pure and undefiled." That was where I had heard the word, during the accident. But what did it mean?

I must have dozed without realizing it. When I opened my eyes, Cynisca was crying.

I sat up startled. She was beside me with her arms wrapped around her legs, head down, as if she didn't want me to see her face.

I reached out and touched her on the arm. "Cynisca, what's wrong?"

She lifted her head with tears streaming down her cheeks. "I can't do it and I don't want to tell you."

"Do what? Why are you crying?"

She turned away. Something or someone had stripped away her confidence and exuberance.

I scooted up closer and touched her arm again. "What? Tell me what you are talking about."

If she didn't tell me soon, I was going to read her mind.

"Daniel, I need to tell you some things. I'm afraid."

"Afraid of what?"

She sniffled. "Hold on, let me get a handkerchief. I'll be right back."

Cynisca walked back inside the house as I sat and waited. I reached for the drink she had brought me earlier. I lifted it to my mouth to take a sip when she screamed, "No, don't drink that."

She ran over and slapped it out of my hand. The contents splattered on the table, the stone slab, and me.

"What did you do, spike it?" I took the towel and wiped off the liquid. The mood had gone from romantic to irksomeness.

"Did you drink any?" she asked. "I don't know what spiked means."

"No, I didn't."

"The drink had something in it that would make you—desire me."

"You mean like Viagra?"

"Like what?"

235

"Never mind. You go from giving me a massage to crying. None of this makes sense."

"It's not what you think. Let me explain. We need to hurry, though."

"Hurry?"

"Let me explain."

I threw the towel on the table. "Go ahead."

"When the two Naser brothers heard your name at the first race, they threatened me."

I stared at Cynisca. "They what?"

"Tariq said you had something they wanted, a scroll or something. I didn't recognize the word they used. Neither brother told me exactly what it was. They just knew you had it, or they thought you had it. They wanted me to find out where you lived so they could search your apartment."

The only scrolls I knew about were the scrolls in Brutus's house.

Cynisca rubbed her eyes. "Tariq said if I didn't find out where you lived, he and his brother would sabotage your chariot, or poison the horses, or do something bad to you."

Cynisca choked up, unable to say more.

I shook my head. I couldn't believe this.

She cleared her throat. "I was afraid. I tried to find out where you lived, but you wouldn't tell me, and I'd tried to follow you home several times, but I always lost you."

"I've never told anyone where I lived."

Cynisca continued. "This is where it gets creepy."

I kept listening.

She sniffled and dabbed her eyes. "An old woman came around a few times after you started racing. I didn't think anything about her until she came up to me and said she knew where you lived.

"I mean, I thought it was strange that some old woman would know, and even if she did, why would she tell me that, unless she knew that I wanted to know, or she knew about the Naser brothers trying to get it out of me, or heard me ask. Look, I don't know, but she gave me the creeps. More than that, she scared me."

I remained silent.

236

"Do you know who I'm talking about?"

I nodded. "Keep going."

"She said she would tell me, but I had to lie with you."

"Lie with me?" I repeated.

"I told her I wasn't that kind of a girl, and—and with you, I mean—" Cynisca averted her eyes. "I'm attracted to you, but—" she swallowed hard before continuing.

"I was afraid that Nidal and Tariq would carry out what they said, and I didn't want you hurt, or the horses. I mean, I love the horses and I care about you."

I nodded.

Cynisca wiped her reddened face with her hand. "I told the old woman that I couldn't. She handed me something and said, 'Put this in a glass of water, mix in a little wine, and it will cast a spell.'"

I looked at the drink that now covered the patio rocks.

Cynisca sniffled and dabbed her eyes again. "I told her no, that I couldn't do that, that it would be wrong. She told me where I could find her if I changed my mind."

"Why? Why would she do that?"

Cynisca stared at me. "Daniel, everyone is out to get you. That happens when you become famous. People want to ruin you, destroy your reputation, take what's yours."

I closed my eyes and remembered—had God been protecting me all along and I didn't even realize it? How else could I explain all the ways I could have been hurt and escaped misfortune? I had been blaming God for my tribulations when I should have been thanking him for his protection.

Cynisca wiped her eyes again. "When you were injured tonight in the race, I panicked. I thought you had died. The brothers had continued to ask about you—they were becoming more aggressive. You and the horses are what I care about."

I stared at the ocean—what about my money?

Clearing her throat, she continued. "I found the old woman and she made me promise—" Cynisca blushed. "You know what I mean, and I went and told the brothers where you lived. We are in their apartment."

"The brothers are at my apartment now? Is that why you brought me here?"

Cynisca nodded.

"I don't know what scroll they are talking about, but they will rob me. I must go, hurry back." I got up, but too quickly and fell.

"Here, let me help you. I don't think they want your money."

The thought of robbery filled me with unimaginable grief. "I've got to hurry."

Unholy thoughts went through my mind as I remembered the demon and the day she saw me enter the apartment.

Cynisca helped me as we hurried through the square. I couldn't run, which made it all seem worse. I rushed as much as I could. When we arrived at the apartment, no one was in the lobby.

We dashed down the hall and found the door ajar. The room was dark and Cynisca lit the lamp. Clothes were scattered on the floor, some personal items I had bought, as well as the few possessions I owned.

I scrambled over to my bed and reached inside the covers. I groped all over and finally ripped everything off the bed. All my shekels were gone. I collapsed on the floor. I didn't recognize my voice—anguished stirrings spewed forth from my soul.

Cynisca put her arm around me and laid her head on my shoulder. "I'm so sorry, Daniel. It's my fault, all my fault."

I don't know how long we sat on the floor. I didn't care that I looked like a fool. Three years I couldn't have back. I had nothing to show for my time here. My dreams of medical school faded.

Maybe I was supposed to take over the family business. Maybe—maybe God was punishing me. I couldn't quit crying. Every shekel I had saved for the last three years was gone.

Anger rose within me. The brothers—how could they do that? And what stupid scroll did they think I have? I knew nothing about a scroll.

I could go back to the brothers' flat and wait for them. They'd have to return sometime, even if not tonight. I could hide inside and confront them when they returned. I looked around the room. My only possession of value was the laurel wreath the young Jewish girl had given me, and my clothes.

Cynisca stroked my arm. "Daniel, you can still run in more races and win more money."

I pushed her away. "Cynisca, I will never race again."

She stared. "What about the contract? You've got another four or five months left."

I looked away. "I can't."

Cynisca shook her head. "I don't understand. How can you walk away now? Don't you want another chance to win more money?"

"I'm going to Jerusalem, to the Passover."

"What about me?" she asked. "I—I'm afraid to stay here. If the old woman finds me and somehow learns that I—that we didn't, what might she do to me? I mean, I know you are going to think I sound weird, but—I'm afraid of her."

How could everything have become so complicated? What could I do to extricate myself from the agreement I had made with Dominus? How could I protect Cynisca? Would I ever be able to escape the demonic woman who had followed me everywhere? How could I give the Naser brothers something I didn't have?

All my money had been stolen and I had run away from the only girl I'd ever loved, and I was stuck in a world thousands of years removed from my home. I had abandoned God for a pagan world and embraced the idolization by adoring fans rather than worshipping the God I once knew. A supernatural being in a chariot of fire had rescued me from certain death and sealed me for a purpose I didn't understand.

I bowed my head in mournful silence, wishing I had made better choices. Why didn't I listen to Simon, the leper? I glanced across the room at the laurel crown given to me by the young Hebrew girl. It glowed with an unnatural light—a light that reminded me of the Merkebah. Hope sprung forth. All was not lost.

While things seemed bad, events could have turned out much worse. I should have died during the race. I could have become drunk with an evil potion and laid with Cynisca. And what did that mysterious man say to me—not to profane my body? I touched the mark on my head. What was the seal he spoke of? I could have gotten Cynisca pregnant. I couldn't endanger her life. Why did I ever make a pact with that witch? She had to be a demon.

I shook my head as the sobering thoughts rattled my soul. Had God sent an angel to spare my life? What had I done to deserve his mercy after turning my back on him? How else could I explain all the things that had happened? I shuddered.

Cynisca's voice cracked. "Are you well? You look like you've seen a ghost."

I turned to her. "We both could be in danger." I knew what I needed to do, but what about her? Cynisca couldn't go with me and she couldn't stay here. I'd never forgive myself if something happened to her.

"Can we take the horses?" I asked.

Cynisca's eyes darted around the room. "I suppose. Why?"

I stood and held out my hand. She scrambled to her feet. "Wait for me. I need to go do something. Stay here, will you?"

"Sure. But tell me about what you want with the horses."

"I'll be right back."

Cynisca relented. "Hurry. I don't like being here alone."

I collected my tunic and cloak and hurried to the door, losing my balance again.

She rushed over to me. "Are you sure you are well?"

"Yeah. I forgot. I'm still having trouble with my balance. I'll be right back." I locked the apartment and went to the washroom and changed. When I returned, Cynisca was gone.

I panicked. When I started to search for her, I heard her. "I'm under the bed."

I looked underneath as she crawled out.

"Why are you under the bed?"

"I don't trust that old woman—or Nidal and Tariq. They told me they were looking for a scroll and they robbed you. What else might they do if given the chance?"

"I've got a plan," I said.

"What?"

I sat on the bed. "I need to go to Jerusalem for Passover. Something happened in the chariot. Something I can't explain. Something I don't want to share right now."

Cynisca nodded. "All right."

240

"But God got my attention, and with all that has happened, I realize—what's important. Things I can't explain, that I can't tell you."

Cynisca looked dejected and lowered her eyes. "What about me?"

"I want to know you are safe. What would happen if I took you somewhere? What about your family, the horses, and Dominus?"

"I'd need to let my family know. As long as the horses are safe—they are worth a lot of money. Dominus—my father would have to deal with him. But you—if they find you, they might send you to the mines because you are an indentured slave, although you've already made so much money, Dominus might let it go. People would be quite upset that a national hero was—treated poorly."

I laughed. "I wouldn't call myself that."

"You gave people hope—every week they had someone they could admire, an escape from Rome, something to think about besides their miserable life."

"Of course, if we take the horses, we will have to return them. Where do you want to go?"

"I have a friend in Galilee who can find a place for you to stay. I want you to go to Galilee, to Brutus's home. Talk to Mari. She's like a governess. Don't talk to anyone but her. Tell her I sent you, that your life is in danger, and can she help you find a place to stay."

"Mari?" Cynisca repeated.

"Yes. You are a skilled horsewoman. I've no doubt you can find work."

"Will you be coming at some point?"

"After Passover, after I visit a friend."

"What is Passover?"

Her question made me stop and think. "You don't know?"

Cynisca shook her head. "No."

"Each year, the Jews make an annual pilgrimage to Jerusalem to commemorate their freedom from Egyptian slavery over a thousand years ago. When they were in bondage, God told the

Israelites to sacrifice a lamb and smear the blood around the doorposts. When Yahweh came to kill all the firstborn in Egypt and he saw the blood, he passed over those homes—hence, the name—Passover.

"I have sinned—greatly, and I need to make things right between God and myself."

"I—I can't go with you?" Cynisca asked.

I shook my head. "No. You wouldn't feel comfortable. Jerusalem will be crowded with Jews for the Passover. They may not welcome you since you are a Gentile. You will be safe in Galilee, away from Jerusalem—and here."

Cynisca studied my room in shambles. "Do you have a girlfriend?"

I rolled my eyes. "Why do you ask me that now?"

Cynisca shrugged. "I don't know. I sense your heart is for someone—else."

I looked away. "It's not relevant right now, so don't worry about it. Understand?"

She nodded. "Yes."

"Now how do we get those horses?" I threw a few things in my bag, along with the laurel crown.

"Is that from last week's race?" she asked.

I shook my head. "Months ago. Someone gave it to me."

"It's beautiful."

"And strange that it hasn't shriveled up like the others," I commented.

Cynisca reached into my bag and pulled out the crown to examine it more closely. "There is something different about it."

"What's that?"

"The color is deep and rich, like the leaves are still living." Cynisca put the crown of laurel leaves back in the bag. "Strange."

I changed the subject. "Can we get the horses tonight?"

"Yes."

"Maybe you can leave a note for your family, but we need to leave—right now."

Cynisca stood. "I'm ready."

I straightened up the room and left the key at the front desk. My bill was paid through next week. I could sell the wreath on the way to Jerusalem to buy a couple of doves as an offering at the temple. I wanted to leave—immediately.

CHAPTER 41 JERUSALEM

W e took the horses from the stables and left Caesarea.
The night was cool and the moon was nine days shy
of being full, but full enough to cast eerie shadows.

Traveling at night now caused me more concern than staying.
That we wouldn't be traveling together made me worry.

Cynisca came up beside me on her horse. "I have an idea."

"What's that?"

"I have a friend down this road. He might be willing to put us
up for the night. He is wealthy—even has a stable for horses."

"Are you sure? I don't have any money."

"I took care of that at the stables."

"What do you mean?"

"I wrote a note that we are hiding the horses for a month for
their protection. Dominus won't question me after what happened
during the race."

"You mean my falling?"

"That and that several gamblers suffered severe losses. This
isn't an honest sport."

"I don't want to know any more," I confessed. "The less I
know the better."

"And one of the slaves found curse tablets in the stall."

"Curse tablets?"

"One of the opposing teams put a curse on you. It had the
whole team spooked—including me. I didn't want to tell you."

"As I said, the less I know the better." Curse tablets—maybe the old woman did that—she had to be a demon.

Cynisca continued. "I also took enough money to provide for the horses' care and I have my own money. I'll lend you some. Just make sure you return Oni in a month or Dominus will come after you—he'll think I made all of this up so you could steal from him."

"What about you and Mosi?" I asked.

"Dominus can't send me to the mines. He needs me as his top trainer. He physically can't do it."

"That's good."

Cynsica frowned. "I wish I knew who that old woman was. She seemed so evil."

"What about the Naser brothers?"

Cynisca thought for a moment "If you aren't racing and they start winning, I think their interest in you will…wane. Money solves many problems. I'm most worried about the old woman."

I didn't want to tell Cynisca that I thought the old woman was a demon. I changed the subject. "Let's stop at your friend's for the night."

Cynisca agreed. "I don't like traveling in this darkness."

We arrived at our destination and Cynisca tied up her horse and walked to the front door. A few minutes later, she waved for me to come.

I dismounted and tied my horse beside Mosi, somewhat skeptical that someone I didn't know would let me stay overnight.

Cynisca smiled as I approached. "Daniel, you will never guess who this is—a mutual friend."

I was greeted by a middle-aged man I didn't recognize, but he seemed to know me.

"Daniel," said Cynisca, "this is Theophilus."

"What?" I stared at the man in disbelief. After a brief pause, we both laughed and received each other in a warm embrace. I couldn't believe we were staying with Theophilus—Dr. Luke's friend. He was the high Roman official who adopted Mari and the same man who asked Dr. Luke if he knew of someone who could help mentor Nathan.

We talked late into the night about Dr. Luke, my work at Brutus's place, how Mari was doing, the healing of Nathan, and why I was no longer needed. Theophilus seemed interested in hearing all about Mari. As is true in small towns, relationships make strange connections.

I was careful to avoid the subject of Brutus's multiple wives, though being a Gentile, he might not have cared. I thought Dr. Luke was Jewish, but perhaps he was only half-Jewish and half Gentile.

By far, Theophilus's greatest interest was in the Jewish rabbi that he called by the Greek name Jesus from Nazareth. When he heard I had met him, he asked me for all the details I could remember.

I told him about Nathan's miraculous healing and raising the dead twelve-year-old girl to life.

He clapped his hands, "Remarkable, remarkable." He looked me in the eye. "Who do you think he is, Daniel from Jerusalem?"

If Theophilus was a pagan, why was he so interested in the Jewish rabbi?

I shook my head. "Honestly, I don't know what to make of him, but I'm on my way to Jerusalem for the Passover and expect to see him. I will come back to Caesarea and give you a full reporting of what I see and hear."

"I'd love to hear your report," Theophilus said. "I am honored to be in your presence anytime. A friend of Cynisca, Mari, and Doctor Luke is a friend of mine."

I thanked him for his kindness.

The slaves took care of the horses and we were given separate rooms. Cynisca confided to me after Theophilus had retired for the evening, "I'd like to learn more about your God, Daniel, and the Jewish rabbi."

I promised her, "After the Passover and my visit to Dr. Luke, I'll make a trip up to Galilee. We will need to return the horses—if the danger has passed for your safety—and mine."

~~*~*

The next morning we left before sunrise. The night's rest rejuvenated my body and I was anxious to get to Jerusalem. Theophilus's passion for spiritual things had quickened my desire to worship in the temple. My life had been spared and I wanted to meet God at Passover.

Even Cynisca's desire to learn more about my God made me realize I was blessed to be a Jew. What I had abandoned was now my burden—my passion. I couldn't wait to offer a sacrifice at the temple.

Soon Cynisca and I came to the fork in the road. She would take the left one and ride towards Galilee. I would take the right one and travel through Samaria towards Jerusalem. My respect for Cynisca had grown—a woman who could have ruined me, who risked her life to protect me.

"Take this money for the care of Oni," Cynisca said, "and here is a little extra for food."

I shook my head. "No, I can't."

Cynisca looked confused. "Why not? You and the horse need to eat. You have no shekels."

I dropped down from the horse and handed her the reins. "Take Oni with you. I will walk to Jerusalem."

Cynisca stared at me. "It will take you days to reach Jerusalem. What will you eat? Why make this harder on yourself than it has to be."

"God will provide for all my needs. I have water."

Cynisca took the reins from me, shaking her head.

I touched her hand. "I'll be fine. There is plenty of room in the stall at Brutus's home for both horses."

"Daniel, I got Oni for you to ride. I trust that you will return him."

I stopped her. "I—I may not make it back. I can't explain now. I want to do the right thing and return Oni to you while I can, and I don't want to owe you or your father any shekels. I must trust God for his provision, and it begins now."

Cynisca studied my face and smiled faintly. "All right."

The sun had risen over the hills. The freshness of the new day was sweet—before the sun's harsh rays brought thirst to the arid land and dust clung to the crowded roads.

The future beckoned us. Circumstances I couldn't have imagined brought us together. How much did God control and how much did I choose? I didn't know.

"I hate long goodbyes," I told her, "but I'll be back to Galilee if God is with me."

Cynisca smiled. "I have a hunch you will come. There is more in Galilee you desire to see than just me."

I laughed. "I have business to tend to, though I fear my heart will be disappointed when I arrive and find the girl I love has married another."

"Daniel, you're alive. Leave to each day its own troubles."

I marveled at her wisdom. Had my own faith in God enabled her to trust in my God, too?

Cynisca pointed towards Jerusalem. "Go to your Passover. Come and share with me about your God. Mine sits on a pedestal made by human hands. Yours occupies a temple—no, more than that. He lives—somewhere up there."

I nodded.

Cynisca smiled. "Well, this is it, I guess. What is that Hebrew word for peace?"

"Shalom."

"Peace to you, Daniel. Shalom." She waved goodbye as she trotted away with Oni beside her.

"Good-bye, Cynisca," I said under my breath.

She looked beautiful on a horse—an expert rider and a woman of virtue.

I wrapped my arms around the laurel crown that had not faded as I turned towards Jerusalem. Then I remembered where I had seen the Naser brother's tattoo. Tariq and Nidal were from the future.

~~*~*

ENJOY THESE BOOKS BY LORILYN ROBERTS

SEVENTH DIMENSION – THE DOOR, VOLUME ONE

2013 Finalist in the International Book Awards, Grace Awards, Selah Awards, and Readers' Favorite. (ages 10 and up)

Seventh Dimension – The Door is the first book in the *Seventh Dimension Series* that combines contemporary, historical, and fantasy elements into a Christian "coming-of-age" story.

A curse put on Shale Snyder because of a secret shrouds her with insecurity and fear. Following suspension from school, Shale's best friend isn't allowed to see her anymore and she feels abandoned by her family. When a stray dog befriends her, she follows it into the woods.

There she discovers a door that leads to another world—a garden with talking animals, demonic underlings, forbidden love, and a king unlike any other. Can Shale overcome her past, defeat the underlings, and embrace her eternal destiny?

AM I OKAY, GOD?
DEVOTIONALS FROM THE SEVENTH DIMENSION

Finalist in the 2014 International Book Awards for best cover design for non-fiction and Christian Inspirational.

Am I Okay, God? Devotionals from the Seventh Dimension answers many questions teens ask dealing with hot topics like self-esteem, dating, bullying, abortion, careers, forgiveness, salvation, and even deeper theological issues related to the end times and the Lord's return.

Woven into the devotionals are stories from the *Seventh Dimension YA Christian Fantasy Series* as well as from the author's life that touch on themes that are important to Christianity and what it means to be born again. Each of the 27 devotionals has a QR code and link to videos, music, and/or books for further discussion and enjoyment.

CHILDREN OF DREAMS, AN ADOPTION MEMOIR

Best-Seller in Adoption Books on Amazon

Inspirational Memoir

"Do you have anything to say?" the judge asked.

My husband, Tim, looked down to hide his shame. "I took away her dreams."

I swallowed hard to hold back tears. After eight years of marriage, supporting him through medical school, and trying to conceive, I couldn't bear the pain of his affair and the divorce he sought.

I left the courthouse where I worked as a court reporter thinking my life was over. I had lost the man I deeply loved and wanted a child more than anything. Now the other woman carried my husband's baby. Jealousy consumed me. Even my friends at church knew she was pregnant before I did. No one told me—not one person. But God did.

I couldn't imagine being single again. I couldn't imagine being happy again. I couldn't imagine ever being a mommy. How could he leave me after all I had done for him? I loved Tim too much to hate him. I felt like a fool for hanging on to broken dreams as my biological clock reminded me each month of my barrenness. Desperation had given way to acceptance of the inevitable, but was God impotent to mend my broken heart? Despite my unbelief, I knew God held the answers to my future. I clung to that as I clutched my Bible and cried.

Twenty-five years later, I wrote *Children of Dreams,* a true story of God's redemption that changed my life—forever!

To learn more about Lorilyn Roberts, you can connect with her on the following social websites.

Lorilyn's website: http://LorilynRoberts.com

http://LorilynRoberts.blogspot.com

Youtube: http://bit.ly/LR_Youtube

Twitter: http://twitter.com/LorilynRoberts

Facebook: http://bit.ly/Facebook_Lorilyn

Authors and bloggers: John 3:16 Marketing Network, visit http://John316mn.blogspot.com

http://bit.ly/John316Network (Facebook)

http://bit.ly/Christian_Books

You can follow the John 3:16 Marketing Network on twitter http://twitter.com/John316Network

hashtag: #John316author

CPSIA information can be obtained at www.ICGtesting.com
Printed in the USA
LVOW07s2026010215

425250LV00001B/304/P

9 781500 785888